W9-CGR-558

A hike in the woods turns into something much more...

Alyce hiked up the gentle incline that led directly to Santanoni's impressive lodge and sat down on the steps to see what was going on out on the lake. . . .

She had been sitting there for perhaps twenty minutes when she heard someone whistling. Then she heard footsteps on the porch of the lodge around the corner from where she sat. Whoever was coming wasn't trying to be quiet. If Max were with her she'd feel a lot more comfortable about being alone—and vulnerable—five miles into the wilderness.

She got up and headed in the direction of the footsteps. They echoed louder as the intruder walked from one section of the labyrinthine porch toward the place where she had been sitting. She rounded the corner at her usual speedy clip and collided with a familiar six-foot frame.

The collision startled her, but Bill steadied her and then maintained his gentle but firm grip on her arm. Ever so slowly he drew her to his steely chest, and she thrilled to the rippling of his arm muscles as he held her to him . . . .

"I'm so glad I've found you here," he murmured into her hair.

CLAIRE M. COUGHLIN and HOPE IRVIN MARSTON write inspirational romance to counteract the immoral and violent nature of contemporary fiction and to present as role models characters who love the Lord. Both reside with their families in New York State.

Santanoni Sunrise

Claire M. Coughlin
Hope Irvin Marston

Heartsong Presents

To my friend and fellow writer, Hope, who taught me the meaning of persistence. (from Claire)

To Gary Provost, mentor and teacher par excellence. (from Hope)

Scripture quotations marked (NIV) are taken from the HOLY BIBLE, NEW INTERNATIONAL VERSION®. NIV®. Copyright© 1973, 1978, 1984 by International Bible Society. Used by permission of Zondervan Publishing House. All rights reserved.

ISBN 1-55748-478-3

SANTANONI SUNRISE

PRINTED IN THE U.S.A.

preface

The construction of enormous estates built in the rustic, "Adirondack style" was once a pastime of the wealthiest families in northeast America. These estates, built from the late nineteenth century until the start of World War I, came to be known as "great camps." Today only thirty-five camps remain, among them, Camp Santanoni.

Camp Santanoni occupies 12,500 acres in the Town of Newcomb, New York, just south of the Adirondack High Peaks. When we visited Camp Santanoni on an outing with the Adirondack Mountain Club, we were impressed by the grandeur of the main lodge, but appalled at the physical condition of that magnificent structure and the other buildings on the estate. After learning the history of the camp, however, we understood why it was in such a state of disrepair.

Our plans to save Santanoni grew out of our discussions with two Camp Santanoni supporters, Dr. Howard Kirschenbaum and Dr. Harvey H. Kaiser. We are indebted to them for sharing their expertise. *Santanoni Sunrise* is an entirely fictitious attempt to create interest and raise support for the preservation of this great camp.

Further information on efforts to preserve Camp Santanoni for the enjoyment and education of future generations can be obtained from the following source:

Adirondack Architectural Heritage
Box 159
Raquette Lake, NY 13436
(315) 354-5832

CLAIRE M. COUGHLIN
HOPE IRVIN MARSTON

one

Rosy tints of dawn ribboned into strawberry rays as the autumn sun ascended over Santanoni Preserve. Alyce stirred in her sleeping bag, but she did not open her eyes. When she awakened several hours later, the sun was shining in her face. She had pitched her tent where she could enjoy the sunrise, and then she had slept through it. She yawned, stretched her slender, lithe legs, and opened one eye to peer at her watch.

"My goodness! Is it really nine o'clock?" That's what she liked about coming to Santanoni. She could relax. She had been coming to this remote preserve for several years, and each time here in the Adirondack wilderness she renewed her physical and emotional strength. Whenever she needed time to think, she and Max, her affectionate old brindled boxer, would desert Syracuse for a few days of roughing it at the great camp. Though threatened by decay and destruction, this former summer estate with its elegantly proportioned lodge had become a sanctuary to her.

Her previous trips had been escape weekends when the responsibilities of nursing became too heavy. She liked being a private duty nurse, but she knew when it was time to back off for a few days of personal renewal.

But this trip was different: She had been given a

mammoth assignment, and she didn't know how to handle it. Camping here beside Newcomb Lake usually renewed her weary mind. This time she hoped it would ease her puzzlement.

She yawned again as she stretched her five-foot frame. Max was nowhere in sight. Not willing to waste such a gorgeous morning sleeping, he was off in the woods creating his own excitement. Alyce vaguely remembered unleashing him when he nudged her in the wee hours of the morning. She had no fear of his running away. He would return once he had made his morning forays.

Her reverie was interrupted by excited yips. Max had probably found a scampering squirrel or a frisky rabbit. Max chased most anything that moved.

"Well, I guess I'd better get out of this sack," she said to the woodland creatures as she shook out her chestnut tresses. It was time for breakfast. Max wouldn't stay away when he smelled her coffee. Coffee meant chow would soon be ready.

She inched her way out of her sleeping bag like a beautiful swallowtail emerging from a chrysalis. After slipping her tiny feet into faded blue Nikes, she walked over to the water's edge to wash her face. Peering at herself in the crystal clear lake water, sparkling dark eyes smiled back at her through mahogany lashes. Her parents must have had those same chocolate brown eyes, she reflected absently. She wished she could remember her mom and dad.

The cold water heightened the dusty rose in her cheeks as it trickled down her short, straight nose. Her lips were full and rounded over perfectly shaped teeth that gleamed as white as the snowy clouds drifting overhead. Though she had recently celebrated her thirtieth birthday, the vision in the lake was one of youthful exuberance, yet at the same time a face endowed with quiet determination, the natural result of having to make important decisions alone.

The sun's rays danced over her dark hair revealing lustrous strands of gold. Though she had hastily tied it in a ponytail before she emerged from her sleeping bag, some escaping wisps charmingly framed her oval face.

Back at her campsite, she pulled out her Peak One stove, pumped it to pressurize the fuel, and lighted it. Next she put water on to boil. She would have enjoyed building her own campfire. She liked the sound of crackling logs and the fragrance of wood smoke, but fires in the forests were dangerous. The stove was faster and it didn't weigh that much.

Coffee first. At home she preferred herbal tea, but coffee tasted good in the fresh air. Then oatmeal. Quick and easy.

Alyce hummed a few bars from her favorite old song, "Liebestraum," as she untied the ropes that secured her food in a tree. She had hung it high to avoid attracting any marauding animal during the night while she and Max slept. A nocturnal visitor would no doubt awaken Max, but protecting her food might prove difficult for him, especially if a black bear wandered into the camp.

When the water began to boil, she poured out enough for her coffee, then she added the oatmeal to the pan.

While it was simmering, she fixed Max's chow. Having returned from his foraging, he wolfed it down and then was off on another excursion.

Suddenly her calm breakfast mood was shattered by a harsh bellow somewhere behind her in the woods.

"Where in thunder did you come from? You shouldn't be running loose in the woods!"

Alyce sucked in her breath. Her body tensed as she heard Max growl. "Max, come!" She whistled for her dog. Her heart thudded in her head as she waited for the inevitable confrontation.

Max bounded into the campsite with the hair on his back standing straight up. He planted himself in front of her. A slow rumble emanated from his throat. Behind him strode a strapping six-foot-tall hiker, a beardless Paul Bunyan with blazing brown eyes.

"This your dog?"

A tremor ran through Alyce when she saw the rippling muscles straining against his shirt and the fire in his eyes. Her pulse quickened. She hoped he didn't sense the fear he had kindled in her heart. He was not someone she'd easily forget.

"Y-y-yes," she stammered.

Max growled again. His protectiveness gave Alyce a scrap of courage. Who was this gruff stranger?

"I'm sorry if he was disturbing you." She didn't feel apologetic, and she refused to be intimidated by this crude woodsman. Though her heart was hammering in her head, she spoke with a controlled voice.

"Listen, whoever you are, you're on my land! I do not

allow dogs to run loose on my property." He paused as if he weren't sure what to say next. "Now what are you doing here anyway?"

Alyce contemplated him as he stood above her like a towering spruce. His muscular arms were bare below mile-wide shoulders. But muscle or no muscle, what right had he to challenge her presence?

"Your land? This land belongs to all of us. There's no sign posted saying dogs must be leashed!" She was surprised at her own boldness, but she kept it concealed from him. "It's really none of your business what I am doing here, but since you asked so politely, I'll tell you anyway. I'm camping out!" She returned his stony gaze.

His brown eyes like bayonets seemed to pierce her heart but somehow she found her voice. Alyce wasn't finished.

"Now, who are you, not that it really matters, and what right have you to disturb us?"

The two stood glowering at one another like eight-year-old ruffians ready to trade punches: the petite brunette with hands on slender hips and the tall, sinewy stranger with furrowed brow and smoldering eyes.

For a few tense seconds their eyes locked. The stranger riveted his gaze on her face. Then ever so slowly he scrutinized her from her ponytail to her faded Nikes and back to her ponytail that rocked gently as she confronted him.

His scathing gaze made her skin prickle. Her cheeks flushed. She felt a tingling in the pit of her stomach. Something about the stranger looked familiar. Was it the dimple on his chin? There was a sensuality about his face that caused her heart to continue its frenzied beating. Nevertheless, his size and demeanor were not to be trifled with. She was glad Max was with her.

Having unnerved her with his impudent assessment, the muscles of his jaw and his face softened. The anger began to fade from his dark eyes like mist dispelled by early morning sunrise.

Alyce studied his face as much as her discomfiture allowed. She wondered why it angered him to find Max and her camping by the lake. Something in those penetrating eyes roused her compassion while making her skin prickle. She sensed he was battling a major problem, and she wanted to help him. Max had stopped growling, but he still stood on guard between them.

"You're right, ma'am." His voice came from a long way off. "I guess this land does belong to everyone . . . now." He gazed out over the lake and then continued. "And, no, there are no posted signs about dogs. I can see you're camping. My apologies."

He went on. "To answer your questions, I'm just walking around m-m-y. . . the estate here." His facial expression had changed from anger to something Alyce could not fathom.

Since he was acting a bit more civilized, Alyce's heart softened. "Do you suppose we could start this conversation again, like civilized human beings? I'm about to make another cup of coffee. Would you care to join me?"

There was an elemental ruggedness about him that suggested he belonged in the outdoors. Yet his skin was light as if he'd spent too many days inside. His dark eyes were a shade lighter than her own while the set of his jaw suggested a stubborn streak.

She wondered why he looked so unhappy. Whatever had triggered his outburst, he seemed harmless. Besides, how could she ignore anyone so ruggedly handsome? Not that she was interested. She neither wanted nor needed a romance in her busy life. Still it wouldn't hurt to be friendly. Whoever this wild creature was, he needed a friend.

The intruder paused before responding. "That's very kind of you, especially after I just bit your head off."

The hint of a smile lifted the corners of his mouth. Alyce smiled in return as she tried to ignore the trickle of interest stirring within her. It was a feeling that she had not experienced since her husband Randy's death. Surprised by her uncontrollable response to him, she averted her eyes.

"I could use another cup of coffee. However," he continued with a sidelong glance at Max, "I'm not sure your dog shares your forgiving spirit."

Alyce glanced down at Max, still standing between them like an armed sentinel, eyes focused warily on the man. His protective rumblings continued. She gave him a pat.

"It's okay, Max." As she spoke to him, the dog relaxed and settled himself at her feet. When she scratched his ears, his stubby tail gave a tentative wag.

The stranger knelt on one knee and held out his hand, palm upward, to Max. "Good boy, Max. Sorry I disturbed you, old fellow. Let's be friends." He talked softly to the boxer.

Alyce smiled at the contrast between this conversation and his earlier harshness when he had discovered Max loose in the woods. *Well,* she thought, *he knows how to greet a strange dog. He can't be all bad.*

Max evaluated the stranger with his big brown eyes. He sniffed his way toward him stretching and retreating like a canine rubberband. Gingerly he touched him. The man talked soothingly to him. When Max licked his hand, he stroked him under the chin and behind the ears. Max's stubby tail began to twitch in acquiescence.

Alyce watched the two get acquainted. Max was a good judge of character. He would sense any hidden aggression. If he trusted this man, then she could trust him too. Still, she wasn't completely comfortable. Where did he come from and why did he object to their camping on Santanoni Preserve?

The stranger surveyed the neat and orderly campsite while he waited for his coffee. Alyce's two-man tent was anchored properly. She had dug a small ditch around it in case of rain. Her food hung high in a tree. His attention was drawn back to his trim hostess. *I bet she doesn't weigh a hundred pounds,* he mused, *and she's not bad looking either.*

Alyce handed him his coffee and invited him to sit on a log nearby. Max settled down between them.

"I'm Alyce Anderson," she said. She smiled at him, trying to ignore the sheer attractiveness of a handsome man in faded blue jeans. She hoped she wasn't blushing.

Silence. Then he cleared his throat and spoke. "I'm

pleased to meet you, Alyce. I'm, uh, uh, my name is Bill, uh, Bill Morgan."

Alyce couldn't help but wonder why he hesitated when telling his name. Reasoning that it wasn't going to hurt to share a cup of coffee with him, she sat down with her cup.

After a few sips Alyce asked, "Did you camp overnight? I didn't see your name in the logbook when we came in yesterday."

All hikers were asked to register in the logbook kept in a small covered cabinet at the trailhead. Such information as your name, the number in your party, your destination and the date was needed to justify expenditures in maintaining the trails.

"No." The frown between his eyes seemed to indicate irritation at her question. There was a long pause before he spoke again. "I'm just in for the day. Do you and Max come here often?" He gave his attention to the dog.

"We try to come up two or three times a year. I love it here. It's peaceful, and the air is fresh. Besides, the buildings intrigue me. I knew the last owners of Santanoni. That's how I started coming here."

Bill coughed as he steadied his shaking coffee cup with both hands. "You knew the last owners of Santanoni?"

"Oh, yes." A smile worked its way across her face as she remembered the Hayeses. "I was Will Hayes's nurse for a while."

"Oh, so you're a nurse? Where do you work?"

"I used to be at Upstate Medical Center in Syracuse. Now I do private duty."

"You say Will Hayes was your patient?"

"Yes. And what a good patient he was. Such a kind man. When he was well enough to leave the hospital, his wife Nellie asked me to come work for them. She was so tiny she couldn't lift Will by herself."

"Why did, mmm, you said her name was Nellie? Why did Nellie have to lift him? Why couldn't he lift himself?"

"Mr. Hayes had suffered several strokes. How fortunate he was to have Nellie to love him and care for him." She paused, reflecting on the beautiful relationship Will and Nellie Hayes had shared. *How wonderful to be so much in love after years and years of marriage*, she thought sadly. For them marriage had been for keeps. They were friends as well as lovers.

Bill's blank expression was a mockery of his true feelings. He had returned to Santanoni to be reconciled with Will and Nellie and he was shocked to learn they weren't there. The condition of his former home was appalling, but he was more concerned with the whereabouts of his parents.

He studied Alyce's countenance as she spoke. Her bright eyes sparkled with animation as she related her tale. Her manner was frank, yet there was no indication she was reaching out to him in anything more than a gesture of friendliness. Now she was telling him Will Hayes was an invalid.

"What happened to the Hayeses? Are they still living in Syracuse?"

Alyce shook her head. "No, I'm afraid not. You see

Will died six months after he was released from the hospital." She paused, remembering the couple who had treated her as their daughter. Will's obviously paternal gestures made her only love him more.

"What about Mrs. Hayes?" The words tumbled out. Too loud. "Is she still in Syracuse?"

Alyce thought it was strange that this man should ask about Mrs. Hayes: Nellie Hayes's death had brought her to Santanoni this weekend.

"Mrs. Hayes passed away two years ago last month." Alyce's eyes glistened with unshed tears.

There was a pregnant silence between them. Then the newcomer spoke again. "You loved the Hayeses, didn't you?"

Alyce nodded as she contemplated her coffee. "I gave up my job at Upstate to care for Will."

"What about Will's family? Couldn't they have helped him?"

Alyce frowned and sighed. Since the man seemed genuinely interested, he might as well know the whole story. "The Hayeses had three children. Their son and daughter were early teenagers when another son was born. They named him Jimmy. They looked upon him as a special blessing from the Lord.

"One day when he was only eight, Jimmy wandered away from the lodge. When he didn't return, the largest manhunt in the history of the Adirondacks was launched. Hundreds of people searched for him."

Alyce concentrated on recalling the events Nellie Hayes had shared with her. "They combed 100 square miles for six weeks without finding a trace of the child. A couple dozen mountain rescue specialists from California came to help as well as crews from the army and the marines. Even the Green Berets helped in the search." She shook her head. "They just couldn't find the little guy."

Bill swallowed often as Alyce recounted the familiar details of the search for his little brother.

"A few years later the older children left Santanoni because of some family disagreements. Neither ever contacted Will or Nellie. What a pity. The Hayeses were beautiful people and they missed their children terribly. After so much heartache at the camp, they moved out and returned to Syracuse."

Bill stared at Alyce as she recited his family's history.

"Will and Nellie were so lonely when I met them. Nellie told me she felt as if all three of their children had died. Will insisted that she get rid of all their pictures. After he passed away, Nellie showed me a photo she had kept. She cried when she got it out of the drawer."

Bill blinked several times. He hoped Alyce didn't notice.

"A few years after the Hayeses left Santanoni, the camp was sold to the New York Nature Conservancy. Later it was purchased by the State of New York. I met Will and Nellie about four years ago. I was just out of training."

At the mention of the estate being sold, Bill gulped. His hands shook and he nearly dropped his cup.

Alyce paused. Perhaps she had talked too much. Well, she couldn't take back her words. Besides, there was no need for her to do that. Whoever this man was, he was not only a good listener, he was also the most handsome man she had met since her husband's death. She brushed an errant curl from her face and winced as a pang of regret over what might have been flitted through her mind.

"Now that I've told you my story, how about yours?" Her eyebrows arched expectantly.

Bill hesitated. He was drawn to this attractive woman, but he was driven by a deeper desire to find out about his family. His eyes darkened when he finally spoke.

"There's really not much to tell." He seemed to be measuring his words against some invisible quota that had been meted out to him. "I've been working for the government in Europe for some time. I just came back a few weeks ago." After a momentary lapse, he asked, "What did you say happened to Mrs. Hayes?"

"Oh. Maybe I didn't tell you. Nothing traumatic. She just lost her desire to live after Will died."

"I see. Well, I really must be going." He handed her his empty cup. "Thanks for the coffee."

The corners of his mouth twitched briefly upward. "How long are you and Max staying at Santanoni?"

"Just a couple of days. I have to be back for work Monday evening."

He looked at her as if he were seeing her for the first time. "I'll be in the area a few more days myself. I'm staying at the Antlers Lodge. Would you let me treat you to dinner before you go back to Syracuse? To make up for my rudeness?"

Alyce's eyes darkened as she tucked in her chin. "Apologies accepted. You need do nothing more." Her response was cool and impersonal. She had answered all of his questions, in excruciating detail, she feared. When she had asked him about himself, he was quick to change the subject.

"Please?" His voice was soft and gentle, almost pleading. "I'm really sorry I shouted at you."

His deep-set dark eyes begged forgiveness. "Can't you stop at the Antlers on your way home? We could have dinner, a lunch, or whatever you wish. Please give me a chance to make amends."

Alyce deliberated. She wished she had never gotten involved with this puzzling intruder. On the other hand, what did it matter? Evident in those dark eyes was a raw hurt, a pain not caused she knew by her presence at Santanoni. Anyway, she'd be needing a good meal before she drove home. Maybe she could find out what his problem was.

"Well, I suppose we could stop." She brushed some stray wisps of hair away from her face as she pondered the invitation. She felt a bit apprehensive but she didn't know why. Was it because there was something familiar about his face? She wished she knew.

"All right. Max and I will stop around one on Monday. It will have to be a quick lunch, though, as I have to get back to my patient."

Bill's lips moved in a semblance of a smile. "Thanks, Alyce. It was a pleasure meeting you. I'll see you Monday. So long, Max."

Alyce watched him as he walked away, his broad shoulders finally disappearing into the woods.

As she cleared away the breakfast trappings, she replayed the morning's encounter. The thought of seeing Bill Morgan on Monday was intriguing, but today she had a problem to solve. She hoped being at Santanoni as the broken bits of summer scattered into the shorter days of autumn would provide the stimulus she needed. Sometimes she wished life would offer her fewer challenges, and today was one of those times. She stowed away her food, whistled for Max, and headed down to the water. A long walk around the lake should give her time to think.

two

Alyce glanced heavenward, noting that the early morning clouds had drifted out of sight. The Lord had given her a perfect day for a hike. As she scanned the skies, her mind drifted back to the summer she met Randy Anderson. It was the summer after her junior year in high school when she was working at the Frosty Shoppe on the edge of Amber Lake.

Randy and his twin brother Rodney were hiking and camping in the Catskill Mountains. This would be their last summer together before their senior year at Albany State. One sticky July afternoon they stopped for a milkshake on their way back to their campsite and Alyce came to the carry-out window to take their orders.

"May I help you, please?" Her innocent smile masked her rapidly beating heart as she stared into identical sets of the most beautiful, bottomless blue eyes she had ever seen.

Two endearing smiles greeted her in return. "Oh, yes. You certainly may," Randy responded with a wink at his brother. His bright eyes sparkled as he gave their orders.

Throughout that summer the twins came often to the Frosty Shoppe. Although they were four years older than Alyce, they developed a close friendship with her. They became the brothers Alyce never had.

Alyce enjoyed the time she could spend with the twins,

but something special was growing between her and Randy. In addition to those compelling blue eyes set in such a handsome face, Alyce was captivated by Randy's zest for the out-of-doors. Here was a man she'd like to depend on, someone to love her and care for her the rest of her days.

When the twins returned to school in Albany, Randy took Alyce's heart with him. Letters from Albany came frequently to Amber Lake that fall, and whenever he could arrange it, Randy came to visit Alyce on weekends. On Valentine's Day weekend he asked her to marry him. A few weeks later he presented her with a dainty solitaire diamond ring. They were married a month after her high school graduation.

Alyce smiled as she recalled her wedding day. Now she had a family of her own! How proud she was of her handsome new husband and his look-alike brother.

Rodney had teased her, "It's a good thing Randy saw you first." His eyes twinkled in merriment. "Otherwise you would be marrying me today."

Alyce glanced at her husband. She wondered what Rodney meant. Randy placed a protective arm around her and glared at his brother with feigned anger. "Tough luck, brother!" he said as he drew Alyce closer to himself.

Rodney kissed her gently on the cheek. "Welcome to our family, Alyce. I'm glad to have you as my new sister."

Alyce blushed. She knew both men loved her, but Randy's love was that priceless love of a man for his wife. Not only did she have a wonderful husband, but she also had a terrific brother-in-law. This was the happiest day of her life.

Rodney's words echoed in her ears as she thought about him. Nine years ago a speedboat driven by a drug-crazed teenager had rammed into Rodney's eighteen-foot Windrose. Randy had been thrown from the boat upon impact and had drowned; Rodney had succumbed while attempting to rescue Randy and Alyce's three-year-old daughter Maria. Upon her release from the hospital, Alyce learned Rodney had named her as his sole beneficiary. She grieved for him as much as for Randy and Maria.

After their marriage Randy insisted that she not work outside the home. "I want you to be waiting for me when I get home from work each day," he told her. When Alyce knew for certain she was carrying his child, she told him. He swung her into his arms and twirled her around the living room.

They could scarcely wait for their baby to be born. The empty nursery began to fill with stuffed animals brought home by a happy father. Little Maria was born on their first wedding anniversary. She had her father's dark hair and the same deep blue eyes. Their joy as husband and wife was complete.

Alyce's thoughts were momentarily swept aside as she took in the glorious day. The trees were already sporting their fall wardrobes. Velvety greens transformed themselves into shimmering yellows and gold, with just a tinge of orange and crimson thrown in. Heralding the arrival of fall, the Creator was wielding with flourish His giant paintbrush.

"Chick-a-dee-dee-dee!" Breaking the natural silence of the forest, a pair of cheerful little black-capped birds chattered loudly as they flitted from tree to tree. A noisy red squirrel squabbled with his neighbors and a blue jay announced his position in an old elm to her left. Alyce studied him for a few moments. Then she walked on through the flowering goldenrod and the New York asters gracing her path amid the abundant seedpods of the summer blooms.

There was so much to enjoy on this trail, but she needed to concentrate on her current problem. She had been asked to do the impossible: to find a way to stop the deterioration of this great camp, Camp Santanoni, and to restore it to its original splendor.

Even if she could figure out a plan, it would be so costly, who could afford to carry it out? Only God in heaven knew how the great camp could be saved. Thus far He hadn't chosen to reveal His plans to any mortal being. One thing was certain. She could always hear Him speak more clearly at Santanoni. She had come asking Him for wisdom and she intended to be tuned in to whatever He answered.

The pungent dry leaves crackled underfoot as she and Max skirted ancient trees that had been hurled headlong across her path by long forgotten winds. Near the campsite the walking was easy, but Alyce knew that would change shortly. She didn't mind. She and Max had made this trip before.

As she scuffled along through the multicolored carpet of leaves, the autumn sun warmed her back and the crisp air put a spring into her step. Her six months' stay in the mountains of Switzerland had shown her that God could restore and renew her broken heart.

As she ambled along the shoreline of Lake Newcomb, her mind wandered back to Randy and Maria. How happy they had been as a family. A smile hovered at the corners of her mouth as she recalled the fun they had camping together.

Her reminiscing was interrupted by a rustling in the leaves. She glanced down to find a pair of chipmunks scampering over a rotten log, their cheek pouches bulging with seeds. They stopped to churr at her. She churred back with her best chipmunk imitation. Then they were off to stow away their loot with Max hot on their trail. It didn't take long for them to disappear, and for Max to return to continue his journey with his mistress.

"You silly dog. You know you can't catch a chipmunk." She stooped down and gave him a pat on the favorite spot on his head.

Maria had loved little creatures in the woods, especially chipmunks. Maybe that was because Randy had bought her a soft cuddly one three months before she was born.

A gentle splash caught her attention and diverted her thoughts. She glanced at the lake but saw nothing. She scanned the water carefully. She guessed who it was playing games with her. Then she saw him halfway across the lake. What looked like a periscope appeared first, followed by a spotted body as the magnificent loon surfaced. Alyce wondered to herself if he would dive again. She knew he would come up quietly where she least expected to see him.

As she watched, the loon began to sink like a submarine, disappearing without a sound. This fellow seemed to be watching something. Instead of submerging himself completely, he lowered only his body and kept his watchful eyes just below the surface. Alyce contemplated the beautiful creature a few minutes and then trudged on.

She considered Nellie Hayes's will. She knew little about inheritances and estates, yet Nellie had requested that she settle her estate in the absence of her estranged children.

Alyce felt a twinge in her heart. She had loved Will and Nellie Hayes. She couldn't imagine why their children had deserted them. She would have given anything to have Randy and Maria back. Although years had passed since their deaths, the memories of the traumatic experience were etched on her heart.

A soft breeze ruffled her ponytail as she walked along. A widow at twenty-one, at first she had clung to her memories of the happy days with her husband and their little daughter. It was her faith in the Lord's ability to supply her needs that enabled her to work through the initial shock. Then came a period of frantic activity that she embraced to keep her mind occupied. When she hit rock bottom, her cousin Barbara convinced her to go to L'Abri.

"You need to put some distance between yourself and the unpleasant memories," she said.

Alyce spent six months at L'Abri in the Swiss Alps. Surrounded by people who loved her and encouraged her, she learned to live again. Her new friends demanded

nothing of her. They were ready to listen or to talk whenever she needed someone near. She spent her mornings
helping with the routine work. In the afternoons she
roamed about, letting the rhythms of God's nature in the
rugged Alps minister to her.

As she wandered about the chalet day after day, the
grief she carried began to dissipate. When she contemplated the majestic mountain paradise in which she found
herself, she felt a calmness in her soul that had fled when
Randy and Maria died. She sensed the orderliness of things
as God had created them. The Creator of such natural
beauty and order could bring peace back into her life too.

When Alyce left L'Abri, it was with gratitude to those
who had helped her. Difficult experiences happened to
everyone. She would accept hers and move on. Coupled
with acceptance came the realization that she could cap-
ture the joy that surrounded her. She would be grateful
for the love of friends and take comfort in the kindness of
strangers. She would forgive the injustices in the world
as well as the people responsible for them. And that in-
cluded the young man who had snuffed out the lives of
those she had loved most. With that forgiveness came
healing.

Alyce decided to become a nurse. She would spend
her time tending the hurts of others. She returned home
and applied for admittance to the fall class at Upstate
Medical Center in Syracuse.

The next few years were busy ones. She applied herself diligently to her studies. She accepted every opportunity afforded her to work in the hospital. At her graduation ceremony, she was awarded the highest academic

honors and shortly afterward the director of nurses at Upstate asked her to work at the hospital.

Alyce met the Hayeses during her first year at the hospital. From their first meeting they filled a void in her life. A compassionate woman by nature, Alyce developed a special fondness for Will and Nellie Hayes. Perhaps it was an innate ability of each to realize the other bore emotional scars that were too painful to be touched.

Her deepening love for them made her think about the parents she had never known. She was grateful to her aunt who had taken her in and raised her when her mother died during childbirth, but she missed having a mother of her own.

Alyce was delighted when after three months Will recovered enough to go home. His doctor told him he could leave the hospital in another week if he secured a nurse to care for him at home. Alyce hoped they would find a nurse who would be extra kind to Will. Being incapacitated was a traumatic expedience, and Will deserved kindness.

Alyce was pleased when the Hayeses asked her to leave the hospital to become Will's private nurse. Private duty nursing would give her more control over her life. She could decide when and where she would work. Besides, if she could make life more bearable for Will, she would do it.

The friendship between Alyce and the Hayes family deepened as the days went by. Nellie liked to talk with her. Now that she worked for them exclusively, they shared many hours together. They discussed most everything, but each respected the other's right not to divulge more than she wished, though each sensed the other was harboring painful memories.

Alyce cared for Will at home for six months until one spring morning he did not wake up. She stayed with Nellie until she had settled matters relating to her husband's death and then she found another patient.

Several months after Alyce had left the Hayeses, Nellie called to ask her to come see her. She greeted Alyce with a warm embrace. There was a mist in her eyes as she poured them each a cup of tea.

"Thank you so much for coming today. And thank you again for being so kind to Will. He loved you as much as he ever loved his own daughter, you know. And I love you just as much, Alyce."

"I'm glad you called. I'm delighted to see you again. How are you doing? Is there something I can do for you?"

Nellie smiled. "Yes, there is. . . . I do hope you won't feel I'm imposing when I ask."

"Nellie, you know there isn't anything I wouldn't do for you," Alyce protested. "What do you need?"

Nellie regarded her thoughtfully. "I don't want to sound morbid, but I'm really looking forward to going to heaven to be with Will. I don't know when the Lord will take me, but I hope it will be soon." Her face glowed as if she were seeing herself with Will standing in the presence of Almighty God.

She continued. "I need to make some revisions in my will. Concerning my property in the Adirondacks. Can you contact my lawyer and set up an appointment at a time you'll be free to take me? I hate to bother you, but since I don't drive, I would really appreciate it."

Alyce remembered how much Nellie hated taxicabs. She'd be glad to oblige her friend.

"Will and I once owned one of the great camps in the Adirondacks," she said. She began to smile as she continued. "It's called Santanoni. That's an Indian word for Saint Anthony. It's a beautiful place. . . ." She paused, envisioning the home she hadn't seen in years.

"We purchased Santanoni at an auction about thirty years ago. The estate covers 12,500 acres. There are two beautiful lakes there, Newcomb Lake and Moose Pond. At one time they were full of speckled trout." Her face contorted. "I suppose the trout are gone now," she said.

"Because of the acid rain?" asked Alyce. She and Nellie had had many discussions about the environment. Since Nellie didn't drive, she seldom left home. But she was an avid reader, and her mind was keen. She kept abreast of current affairs.

Nellie nodded. "Let me tell you about Santanoni. There are two mountains nearby, Moose and Baldwin. They're not tall enough to belong to the prestigious 46ers, but they are great for bushwacking." Her eyes twinkled at some memory. "Will and I loved to hike those mountains. We spent days tramping about just enjoying the mountains. . . and each other. . . . " Her voice trailed off into the air.

Alyce wanted to learn more about Santanoni. She and Randy had enjoyed camping in the Catskills but she didn't know anything about Adirondack camping.

"Santanoni sounds like a lovely place. Did you have a log cabin in the center of that big estate?"

Nellie chortled. "A cabin? Well, I'd hardly call it that though it was built with 1,500 logs. There was a main lodge in the center of a cluster of buildings. It had six sprawling buildings under one roof. The buildings were tied together with a system of porches. We had eighteen bedrooms in our lodge."

Alyce's eyes widened as Nellie described Camp Santanoni. This was no ordinary little mountain retreat.

"The lodge was flanked by a lovely artist's studio. And there was a boathouse too."

Alyce tried to picture Santanoni as Nellie described it to her. "It sounds like a marvelous place," she said. "I'd love to see it."

"There's no reason why you can't," said Nellie. Her voice had gained its former determination. She went on to describe two other clusters of buildings: the gatehouse complex in the hamlet of Newcomb and the farm complex about a mile north of the gatehouse on the trail to Newcomb Lake.

Without telling her why, Nellie said she and Will had sold the estate. "We had a tragedy in our family, Alyce . . . ." She grimaced. "Actually it was the first of several tragedies. That's what brought on Will's first stroke, I think. We couldn't go back to Santanoni after so much heartache. We decided to sell the estate and try to forget the unhappiness we experienced when we lived there."

Alyce listened intently as Nellie spoke of things she had kept hidden in the recesses of her heart.

"Once we moved out of Santanoni, we never went back. We read in the newspaper that the Conservancy Committee resold Santanoni a year later to the State of New York.

It became part of the great Adirondack Forest Preserve. Once it became part of the preserve, it was opened up to hikers and campers. I don't know what it is like now." She gave a long, pensive sigh. "I hope someone is taking good care of it. I'm sorry the Nature Conservancy didn't keep it."

"Why, Nellie? To keep the public out?"

"Oh, no, Alyce. Quite to the contrary. Once Santanoni became part of the Adirondack Park, the 'Forever Wild' clause prevented the state from maintaining or using the camp. I shudder to think what the camp must look like now. It hurts to think of those grand structures standing there deteriorating through mandated neglect."

Alyce sensed the pain these remembrances were eliciting for Nellie. She loved her. She wanted to assuage that heartache if she could. Suddenly she had an idea.

"Nellie," she asked, "would you like me to take you to Santanoni?" She wasn't sure just when she could do that, but somehow, for Nellie's sake, she'd do it. Besides she'd like to see the camp too.

Nellie's eyes brimmed with tears as she took Alyce's hand and gently squeezed it. "Oh, you dear, dear girl. Thank you for your offer, but I could never go back to Santanoni. . . except in my memories. I wouldn't go now that Will is gone. Besides, I couldn't go. It's a five-mile hike into the camp. You can't drive into Santanoni Preserve. Motorized vehicles are not permitted there."

She looked at Alyce. "I have my memories. Some good. And some not so pleasant. That's sufficient. Now if you'll arrange for me to see my lawyer, I shall be grateful."

Alyce arose. She gave Nellie a hug and left, a woman on a mission. First she would arrange for Nellie to visit her lawyer. Then she would check her own schedule. She intended to see Santanoni Preserve for herself.

three

Alyce delighted in the late summer flowers blooming along the lakeshore. The lavender wild asters. The yellow goldenrod. The white Queen Anne's lace. Though their colors were fading, their beauty lingered to be enjoyed briefly before the onslaught of winter changed the landscape to a dull grayish brown.

As she meandered along deep in thought, Alyce glanced down. The sandy beach was imprinted with delicate Vs, sure proof that deer had left the cover of the deep woods to venture down to the shore to drink. They could do that safely now that most people had gone from the lake.

A slapping in the water diverted Alyce's attention and she glanced up in time to see a beaver. Max heard him, too, but he never pursued animals in the water.

Alyce smiled at the sight of another wild animal. How she wished she could see one of the lynxes that had been released in the Adirondacks the past spring. She'd love it if one of their summer kittens should wander down from Baldwin Mountain in search of adventure. But that was expecting too much.

The animals, she knew, had already recognized that change was in the air and were preparing for it. Likewise people needed to accept changes in their lives. She walked on, continuing her thoughtful journey.

She had taken Nellie to see her lawyer. Then, without telling Nellie, she had taken her first free weekend to go to Santanoni. She had little difficulty finding the trailhead once she got to Newcomb. The five-mile hike into the camp was a delight, but she was unprepared for the dilapidated buildings. Her heart sank at the sight of the once magnificent lodge standing like a weary vagrant on a deserted street corner, its shadowy veranda now the property of barn swallows.

As she picked her way through the fragrant balsam and Lapland rosebay threatening to hide the stone steps leading down to the lake, Alyce knew she must never tell Nellie what she had discovered. Her heart would break at the thought of her beautiful home in such a neglected state.

The next time she could get away she went to the village authorities in Newcomb to find out why the great camp was not being cared for. The Newcomb postmistress was the first to tell her about the disappearance of the Hayes's son, the first tragedy.

Alyce's heart ached for the Hayeses. Their grief had been so deep that even years later they still could not talk about it with her. She had never told them about Randy, Maria, and Rodney.

Nellie never discussed the disagreements that caused her children to leave home. Alyce wondered what had been such a big issue that they could not resolve it. The tragedies in her own life had taught her that we should cling to our families for as long as we have them.

After Nellie's death, Alyce cared for a number of patients. Though her insurance money from Randy and Rodney had left her financially independent, she continued working. She liked private duty nursing because she could choose her patients and her schedule was flexible.

Two years later she received a letter postmarked Newcomb. She inspected the envelope. Although she had returned to Santanoni to hike a number of times, she had never met anyone in Newcomb except the postmistress. She glanced at the return address.

An attorney's office? She knew no attorney in Newcomb. She ripped the letter open and scanned it hastily. She blinked, sat up straighter, and read the letter again. The letter simply stated that she, Alyce Anderson, R. N., of Syracuse, New York, had been named the executor of the will of Nellie Hayes. Would she, as soon as possible, make an appointment to meet with the lawyer to expedite the conditions of the will?

She had called the attorney, a Mr. Roberts, but his secretary was unwilling to discuss the matter over the phone. It was mid-August before she was able to get away. Her plan was to drive up in the morning, meet the attorney in the late afternoon, spend one night in Newcomb, and return the following morning.

Alyce paused to scan the lake. She was hoping to see more loons. The babies would be a couple of months old now and no longer chicks but large grayish birds that looked out of place behind their speckled parents. Instantly she pictured Maria, jumping up and down when she saw a loon chick riding piggyback on his mother's back.

Randy had explained to her that the little loons could become watersoaked if they stayed in the water too long. When they rode on their parent's back, they were safe from large fish and snapping turtles that would have gobbled them up for lunch. The whole family had been excited the day they saw two chicks riding on their mother's back.

There would be no hitchhikers this late in the fall. If they tried it, the chicks would swamp the parent and find themselves back in the water. Though she looked carefully, Alyce saw nothing on the lake other than an occasional fish jumping. She trekked on.

By now she was replaying her visit to the attorney's office. She parked her car in front of the library and walked across the street to a modest white ranch-style home with green trim. A neatly lettered sign on the front lawn, surrounded by brown and yellow chrysanthemums, declared the law practice of one Robert D. Roberts.

Soft chimes from the doorbell drifted out from the open window. The door was opened promptly by a petite, blue-eyed blond.

"Hello! Please come in. You must be Ms. Anderson. I was just leaving."

Before Alyce could say more than "Good afternoon," the woman was out the door and halfway down the sidewalk. Alyce looked around. She found herself in a well-appointed, cozy sitting room. Its accents of yellow, green, and orange reflected good taste as well as warmth.

Suddenly but unobtrusively a man of medium height and build appeared. His charcoal pin-striped suit, immaculate white shirt, and green and maroon tie were worn with the casual style of a man whose life is in order.

"Good afternoon," he said, extending his hand. "I'm Rob Roberts." His lips curved and a smile crinkled his eyes. "You must be Alyce Anderson."

"I'm pleased to meet you, Mr. Roberts. Yes, I'm Ms. Anderson."

They shook hands and he gestured toward a chair. "As

you can see, I have my office in my home. I hope you'll feel comfortable here." He seated himself behind his desk. "My secretary will be back momentarily. May I offer you something to drink? You must be tired after your long drive from Syracuse. Coffee? Iced tea? A ginger ale? Or perhaps you'd prefer something a bit stronger?"

Alyce winced. His familiarity sent her adrenalin coursing through her body. "No, thank you." She didn't meant to sound so curt. "Frankly, I'd like to get down to business right away if we may." She was coloring her words with neutral shades.

"Certainly, Ms. Anderson." He had picked up her signal. He offered her a weak smile and reached for a folder on the corner of his desk.

At least he has the decency not to call me by my first name, Alyce mused. She felt uncomfortable.

"As my secretary informed you, you have been named the executor as well as a beneficiary in Mrs. Hayes's will." He retrieved his glasses from his pocket, put them on, and opened the folder. "Mrs. Hayes was my client when I lived in Syracuse a few years ago," he said. He handed Alyce a document. "Here is a copy of the will."

Alyce scanned the lengthy document and handed it back to the lawyer. "Mr. Roberts, this will states that the inheritance shall go to the Hayes's children, William and Elisabeth. They are the heirs, not I. The estate belongs to them."

The attorney smiled and shook his head. "No, Ms. Anderson. If you read more carefully, you'll see that the children have forfeited their inheritance. The will states that if they do not try to contact their parents within two years of Mrs. Hayes's death, they will lose their rights as heirs. The estate becomes yours to settle. Twenty-five thousand dollars goes to you personally. The remainder, about one hundred thousand dollars, is to be used for the preservation of Camp Santanoni."

The attorney sensed that Alyce was having difficulty grasping the enormity of the inheritance. He continued. "I haven't seen Santanoni, but I would be delighted if you would permit me to take you there." It was a statement, not a question.

"That will not be necessary," Alyce said, rising from her chair. "I've been there a number of times. Thank you for the appointment, Mr. Roberts." She extended her hand, not because she wanted to, but because courtesy dictated that she do so. As he took her hand in both of his, she felt red color creeping up her neck.

"Please call me Rob. It was a pleasure to serve you. Do let me know if there is anything else I might do for you. I'm at your service." He did not release her hand as he smiled directly into her eyes.

Alyce disengaged herself from his grasp, embarrassed by his unprofessional conduct. "Thank you, Mr. Rob. . . uh, Rob. . . ."

She was freed from the lawyer's attentions by the ringing of the phone. Since his secretary was out, he had no choice but to answer it himself. As he did so, Alyce made her escape, her face flushed with displeasure.

Safely seated in her red Escort, she rested her head on the steering wheel. Nellie's will was a surprise, and that lawyer was too friendly. She shook a thick swatch of brown hair off her shoulder and tried to clear her head. A slow smile etched its path across her face. Then she began to laugh. The idea was ludicrous. Why would

Nellie Hayes leave $25,000 to her? And how could she ever carry out Nellie's wishes for Santanoni?

She thought about her relationship with Will and Nellie. They never flaunted their wealth though she knew they were people of means. They lived in the valley in a home filled with fine furniture. Not everyone could afford a private nurse. Still the value of their estate boggled her mind. She needed to find a place to think. She turned the key in the ignition and headed back to the room she had secured at the Antlers.

Back in her room she read the will again and again. She wondered what had happened to the Hayes's children. Even when writing the will, Nellie had hoped they would return. She had given them two years to show up, and they hadn't come.

Alyce spent a restless night, her brain operating in overdrive. What she needed was a day at Santanoni, but she had to be back by six to relieve a nurse now on duty for her.

She got up at sunrise, packed her few possessions in her overnighter, paid for her lodging, and headed back to Syracuse. She would eat breakfast enroute. Perhaps she'd be able to formulate a plan on her long drive home.

She was committed to caring for Mrs. Martinez through Labor Day weekend. The first weekend after Labor Day she and Max could go to Santanoni for three days. That should give her enough time to come up with a solution. Besides, Max would love three days at the camp.

By now Alyce and Max were three-quarters of the way around the lake. *Okay, Alyce,* she chided herself. *You've spent all of this time looking back. Now you must move ahead. Just what are you going to do about Santanoni?*

For the hundredth time she contemplated the provisions of the will. Nellie was asking her to take the bulk of the estate to preserve Santanoni. That meant finding a means that met the conditions of the "Forever Wild" clause. Nellie had told her it was assumed that Santanoni came under that clause that doomed it to destruction by natural forces. But what if that assumption were wrong?

She had prayed asking the Lord to give her wisdom to know what to do. Now a plan was forming in her mind. When she and Max got back to Syracuse, she would contact her friend Joe Heisler, a state senator in Albany. Joe could find out what she needed to know about Santanoni. He might have some suggestions on how the money could be used to stop the deterioration.

For one thing the lodge roof needed to be fixed immediately. Anyone could see that. Some of the smaller buildings were beyond repair, but not the magnificent lodge. The gatehouse was in pretty good shape. So was the milkhouse. But the others. . . . Preserving Santanoni would require the expertise of a restoration architect. She was sure of that.

She would find a way to do it for Will and Nellie. . . and for Randy and Maria and Rodney. A restored Santanoni would be her monument to the five people she had loved and had lost.

She had been so engrossed in her thoughts, she didn't realize they were almost back to their campsite. Max had tired of his forays. He was nearly twelve now, after all, and his weary legs had dictated he stay beside her for the last mile.

Alyce had a late lunch and then headed down to the beach. The warm afternoon sun would be pleasant. She was relieved that she had reached some conclusions. She stretched out on the beach and soon she and Max were fast asleep. They missed a pair of majestic loons paddling by, their still earthbound chicks in tow.

four

Instead of heading back to the main lodge, Bill bush-whacked his way through the brush to the deserted studio. A wan smile crossed his face. So Will and Nellie were dead. Will and Nellie, not Mom and Dad. He had started calling his parents by their first names in his early teens. A form of rebellion maybe, but the names had stuck. Well, one more regret to add to his growing list.

He had made three trips into the camp since his return from Europe, each more painful than the previous one. He was aggrieved to see the devastation of what had been such a well-kept estate. A lump was forming in his throat, and no matter how often he swallowed it wouldn't go away. He eased himself down on the steps of the abandoned studio.

His thoughts drifted back over the years to his heated discussions with his father. Unlike his father and grandfather, he had never been interested in stocks and bonds or other financial dealings. They had made good investments and as a result they lived well. Thus when Camp Santanoni came up for sale, they had the cash to buy it. They wanted Bill to follow in their footsteps. To carry out their plans. To pursue their dreams.

But Bill was interested in buildings, not bonds. He wanted to design and create out of wood and stone. For a time he thought he'd become a carpenter. As he grew older, he developed an appreciation for the fine buildings

44

at Santanoni. Maybe he would become an architect.

He was fascinated by the huge lodge. Whoever had built it was a master builder. At one time he and his sister decided they would count the black logs to see if there really were 1,500 in the building. They gave up soon, but Bill continued to admire the sound construction and the seeming indestructibility of the sprawling building.

As a child he played with his father's prize Jerseys in the meadow or the barn. When he tired of that, he walked across the road to watch the men working in the milkhouse. As he grew older, he learned to appreciate the beautiful studio, the little cottage with its cathedral window overlooking the lake and the mountains. The studio was also his sister's favorite hideaway, and the two of them spent hours there playing together. Afterward Bill would head back to his room in the lodge and reconstruct the building on paper.

His infatuation with architecture continued into high school, that is, until he developed an interest in girls and sports. He still dabbled with his designs of miniature buildings, however, and he kept abreast of the financial world, mostly to please his family.

When he registered for his freshman year in college, he chose a career in liberal arts. Because his mother was French Canadian, Bill had been brought up speaking two languages. When a certain Puerto Rican beauty sent his pulse rate skyward, he decided first to study Spanish, and then to follow her major, political science. By and by the lovely young woman went her way, but Bill was hooked on the machinations of politics throughout history.

When his parents cut off his financial aid following a bitter dispute concerning his future, his grandmother

Willa, for whom he was named, came to his rescue. She paid his tuition and gave him a monthly allowance that permitted him to continue his studies at New York University.

Things seemed to go well for him after he received his degree. He became an aide in the office of a senator, and eventually he applied for a position in the diplomatic corps. Empowered by his quick grasp of foreign languages, his photogenic mind, and his winsome personality, he quickly rose through the ranks. But there was an emptiness in his life that he couldn't satisfy. Although he dated some pleasant women, he did not meet anyone he wanted to marry.

Ever since he had arrived in Europe he had kept journals, and the thought had been growing in his mind for some time that what he had written was marketable. Maybe it was time to go home, back to Santanoni, to make peace with Will and Nellie. There in the quietness of the great camp he could edit his journals for publication.

What fools we were, he lamented, thinking of both his sister and himself. *Why did I wait so long to come back?* The lump in his throat was growing. *How am I ever going to explain everything to Bette?* He didn't even know where his sister lived. How much grief had he caused his parents? He sank to the steps. The tears he'd not yet been able to shed finally were released. He'd been a rotten son and a lousy brother. If only he could start his life all over again. . . .

He sat on the steps a long time reviewing his life and regretting his failures. Finally he made his way back to his rented Lincoln Continental parked beside the red

Escort. Now he knew who owned that car. She had fooled him. He assumed Max was her male companion when he saw the names in the logbook. He frowned and shook his head. He unlocked his car and slid behind the wheel. The five-mile hike back from the lodge had done little to lift his burden of discouragement and frustration.

His troubles buzzed through his aching head like bees swarming in May. He continued to berate himself silently. *You come home to find campers are enjoying your family's estate. The buildings you loved are inhabited by spiders and mice. A stranger tells you your parents have died heartbroken and your home has been sold to the State of New York.*

He shuddered as he thought about the "Forever Wild" clause. It would tie the estate into legal knots that only a Houdini could untangle. *I'm glad I didn't give that woman my full name,* he mused, but he was having second thoughts. *I didn't really lie about my name. I just didn't tell her the whole truth.* But deep inside he knew better. He scowled as he turned the key in the ignition and backed out of the parking lot.

Alyce glanced around the campsite. She wanted to make certain she was leaving nothing behind except her footprints. "If you carry it in, carry it out." That was the motto of every bona fide lover of the wilderness and she subscribed to it.

She took one last look at the lake. She wanted to remember it as she had seen it at the break of dawn when the mist was gently rising. She was disappointed that no loons had awakened her with their eerie yodels during the predawn hours. Still the quiet beauty of that

September morning had refreshed her. She was leaving
Santanoni renewed in spirit.

She gave Max a pat. "Okay, ol' pal. It's time for your
load." The dog pranced about while she adjusted the
straps on his backpack that fitted over his muscular back
like miniature saddlebags. His stubby tail twitched. He
carried his little load as though he enjoyed it.

"There you are, Max. Now just give me a minute to
get into mine."

She set her pack on a stump and stooped down to ease
into it. No newcomer to a backpack, she had learned to
carry only necessities when she and Randy backpacked
into the Catskills. Squaring her shoulders, she shifted her
pack, adjusted the straps, and picked up "Wally," her
walnut walking stick.

"Okay, Max. We're off."

It was almost one o'clock when Alyce parked her
Escort wagon in the lot behind Antlers Inn. Max roused
himself hoping to be let out.

"No, Max. Stay! Sorry, but you can't come this time."

Retrieving her lipstick from her purse, she passed the
carnation pink tube over her mouth. She anchored her
ponytail with a pink bandana and tucked her checkered
shirt into her jeans. She tried to brush aside what she was
feeling about Bill Morgan. So what if he's got magnificent muscles and an impregnable wall for a chest? Without intending to do so, she was giving her heart a little
slack.

She rolled down the windows so the boxer would have
plenty of air, gave him an affectionate pat on the head,
and slipped out of the car. The butterflies in her stomach
began a delicate ballet. She took three deep breaths and

walked into the inn.

Bill was sitting at a corner table by the window having an animated chat with the waitress who was obviously enjoying her attractive guest. The rich outlines of his shoulders strained against the blue plaid fabric of his flannel shirt while wisps of curly brown hair crept out from under his collar. Draped across his shoulders was an azure blue V-necked sweater. He took a casual sip of iced tea as he listened to the waitress.

Something about those rugged features looked familiar. Mahogany eyes. Aquiline nose. Firm and sensual lips. Teeth white and even. Chin dimpled and determined. A wan shaft of sunlight struck his thick, dark hair making it gleam like burnished gold. Where had she seen this man before?

She reminded herself that she wasn't looking for romantic involvement. Randy was the first and only man in her life and after his death she thought she wouldn't exist without him. Now she suffered only occasional bouts of loneliness, usually late at night. She never considered loving another man. Now Bill unconsciously was reminding her how empty her nights had been since Randy's death.

As she entered the dining room, Bill dismissed the waitress with a polite but firm, "Excuse me, please," and rose to greet her.

"Hello, Bill." There was more warmth in her voice than she intended. "It's nice to see you again." The waitress melted away, her face reflecting envy.

"Hello, Alyce." He gave her a gentle smile that sent her pulse racing. "I was afraid you wouldn't come." His dark eyes softened as they looked into her face. "I can see why you wear pink."

"Thanks. You don't look too bad yourself. I love your sweater. Is it handknit?"

"Yes, it is. I bought it in Switzerland last winter."

"Oh, you've been to Switzerland too?" Alyce chided herself silently at the obvious redundance of that statement.

Sensing her embarrassment, Bill went on. "How was your weekend at Santanoni? Did you come upon any more bullies?"

Why did he change the subject? she wondered, slightly irritated. *Why won't he talk about himself?* "Max and I had a great time." Her voice held a slight edge as she spoke. She took a deep breath. "And how about you?" She didn't intend to pry, but she was curious to know why he was staying at the Antlers.

A slight hesitation shaded his eyes. "Oh, I haven't done much since Saturday." He paused like a chess player weighing his next move. Then he continued. "I have some business in Syracuse that I must tend to in a week or so."

"You do?" Alyce wished she hadn't sounded so enthusiastic. *What would he think?*

Her quick response was not wasted on Bill. His deep brown eyes gleamed. "Could we get together when I'm in your fair city?"

"I guess so." It was Alyce's turn to be surprised. Why would he want to see her again? Not that she minded.

The waitress returned to take their orders. Their lunches were served promptly and they chatted amiably over their egg salad sandwiches. Each one carefully avoided anything too personal.

Alyce related some of her camping experiences with Max. Bill spoke of having some business dealings in Syracuse, but he did not elaborate despite Alyce's subtle probing. His brief, vague comments annoyed Alyce.

"Do you go to Syracuse often?" She hoped her tone sounded impersonal.

"No." His tone implied that she should not ask anything more. But she did not give up easily.

"How long do you plan to be in Syracuse this time?"

"I'm not sure, Alyce."

She tried switching topics. "How long were you in Switzerland?"

He hesitated before responding. Looking into her eyes, he said softly, "For about six months. But let's not talk about me. I'd rather talk about you." He disarmed her again with his smile.

Lunch soon ended and it was time for them to go their separate ways. Alyce had a long drive ahead of her. As she rose from the table, her arm brushed her glass, spilling the water. She grabbed her napkin to catch it before it drenched Bill. Since he had risen with her, little splashed on him.

"Ooooooooh!" Alyce was mortified. "I'm so sorry. Are you all wet?"

Bill chuckled. "Now that's what I call a personal question." His dark eyes danced but he added gently, "Relax, Alyce. It was an accident." He was sorry he had teased her.

The waitress came to their rescue. They thanked her with a generous tip and left the dining room together with Bill's arm gently encircling her waist.

"I'd better say goodbye to Max," he said. "I'd like to

stay on friendly terms with him."

He patted Max. "So long, boy. See you again some-time, I hope." Max rolled his dark eyes at him, licked his hand, and wagged his tail.

"I'll call you when I get to Syracuse." It was a promise gently spoken. Not trusting herself to respond verbally, Alyce smiled and nodded.

She put the car in reverse and slowly backed out of the parking lot. She studied him a moment through her rear-view mirror then she pulled onto the highway and headed west to Syracuse.

five

The phone jangled impatiently as Alyce shuffled her bag of groceries so she could unlock the door. Why did that lock always stick when she was in a hurry? She tried it a second time. The lock wouldn't budge. Finally the door swung open but by the time she picked up the receiver, the caller had hung up.

Who was calling at that hour? Someone who knew her schedule well, or a stranger taking a chance that she would be home for the dinner hour? She hoped it was Bill Morgan. He had said he would call.

She deposited her groceries on the kitchen counter and dialed her landlord's number. Mr. Jameson promised he'd stop by the next day and fix the lock. He could fix anything. Whenever he came to Alyce's apartment, Sarah, his vivacious wife, came along.

"I don't trust him out alone," she said with a wink at Alyce the first time they came. However, it was soon apparent that the love between the two was on a firm foundation. Sarah came because she was hungry for "woman talk." While her husband tended to whatever needed fixing, she and Alyce visited over a pot of herbal tea.

Alyce was the Jamesons' favorite tenant. She had occupied one of their apartments ever since coming to Syracuse to begin her nursing training. They admired her spunk and went out of their way to encourage her in any way they could. Alyce knew the lock would be fixed by the time she got home the next day.

She eyed the kitchen clock as she put away her groceries and fed Max. She wondered again if Bill had tried to call. She hummed a snappy tune as she fixed herself a light supper.

Her patient had needed so much attention that day that she scarcely had time to catch her breath. After a brief debate with herself, she opted for a quick shower instead of a relaxing soak in the tub. She didn't want to miss another call.

She threw on an old sweatsuit and toweled her hair, finally brushing it back into a ponytail. Suddenly the doorbell rang. She slipped her damp feet into black slippers and hurried to the front door.

A smile lit her eyes as she looked through the peephole. Flinging open the door, she greeted her old friend Joe Heisler. "What a nice surprise!" Joe clasped her in a warm embrace.

"Hello, Alyce. I hope you don't mind an unannounced caller. I was in the neighborhood and thought I'd stop and answer your questions in person." His eyes reflected admiration as he released her. "I tried to call you earlier, but I didn't catch you in."

"Well, come on in. May I fix you a cup of coffee?"

"That would hit the spot. Thanks."

Alyce plugged in the coffee pot and got out two cups. She didn't like coffee in the evening, but she remembered that Joe did.

"How are things at the Statehouse? Are you as busy as ever in Albany?"

"Now that's an understatement, Alyce. We're trying to get things sewed up so we can go home for Christmas recess." A smile edged up the corners of his mouth as he thought about his work. He had represented his legislative district well for six years, due primarily to the personal interest he took in each one of his constituents. His visit to Alyce's home was typical of his homespun style.

He looked at Alyce with questioning eyes. "How are things with you, Alyce? Is everything all right? Are you happy?"

Alyce knew his questions were prompted by a genuine interest in her welfare. After the death of her husband, he had hoped for a deeper relationship, but when he realized she wasn't interested, gentleman that he was, he backed off.

Alyce had followed his legislative career through the media. He had a reputation for honesty and integrity. When she returned from her weekend at Santanoni, she had written him to find out how to carry out the wishes of Nellie Hayes. She was pleased with his prompt response.

"Max and I are doing all right," she said studying her hands. "I get lonesome sometimes, but we make out okay. Right now I'm so concerned about Santanoni and Mrs. Hayes's will. I spend most of my waking hours wondering how to proceed."

She didn't mention the part Bill Morgan was playing in her drama. Her agitated emotional state was in large part due to him.

Joe glanced at his watch. "I will come right to the point. I'm sorry, but I have an appointment at eight, and I won't be back in Syracuse for two months."

His deep blue eyes sparkled as he surveyed her again from ponytail to slippers. She sensed his quickening pulse and she felt her own breath quicken and her cheeks flush.

She needed to divert his attention, and fast. "What did you find out? Is Santanoni doomed to destruction because of the 'Forever Wild' clause?"

A slight frown darkened Joe's countenance before he responded. "Not really, though for a time it was assumed that it came under those restrictions. You can thank our governor for signing a bill to save historic structures in the forest preserve like Santanoni. The law requires that an advisory committee inventory such structures. That law also allows the state to maintain places like that great camp."

Alyce interrupted. "Then we don't have to worry. If the law says it can be maintained, we just need to find the financial resources to maintain it!"

"Wait just one minute. Have you any idea how much it would cost to restore those buildings? They've been sitting there decaying for twenty years. Besides that, the new law may be challenged as unconstitutional by environmental groups."

Alyce frowned and sighed. Nothing was ever easy in this world. "Tell me, Joe, do you honestly think there is a way to save Santanoni?"

It was Joe's turn to sigh. He captured her eyes with his and she felt the color rising once again in her cheeks. She instinctively lowered her thick brown lashes. She wished he wouldn't look at her that way.

After what seemed like an eternity, he asked, "How important is it to save Santanoni? How hard are you willing to work? Do you have the time and the patience to work through the legalities? And once the legal hurdles are overcome, what about the finances? Do you have some rich uncle with treasure-laden ships ready to dock at your port?"

Alyce knew that Joe was only helping her see that she was contemplating a gargantuan task. She wasn't a quitter, but she wasn't indefatigable either.

Joe continued. "I'm not trying to discourage you." He smiled again. "I just want to make sure you understand the obstacles in your path. "

He hesitated a moment and then spoke as though he were weighing each word before letting it escape. "I doubt that you or any other woman could accomplish such a task alone. If you would like me to work side by side with you, I could. . . ."

Alyce cut off his words with a nod. She knew what Joe was hoping for, but she wasn't interested in that kind of partnership. "Thanks, Joe. I'll find a way to save Santanoni. I appreciate your taking time to help me understand the obstacles in my path."

Joe glanced at his watch again. "There are a few more things you should know, then I must be going." He settled back into his chair and continued. "I don't know what your plans are for Santanoni, but you need to have something definite in mind. Legally the camp can't be leased for private enterprise. That would certainly be challenged. It's possible that it could become a center for interpreting the Forest Preserve to the public."

Alyce readjusted her cushion as Joe explained.

"Maybe it could become a hostel for campers and hikers. It could offer a crackling fire, a warm meal, and a dry bed. Or perhaps educational programs could be presented there for the public."

"Could it be leased to a private group like the Adirondack Mountain Club for a wilderness lodge?"

"That too might be possible. The big problem is that no one, or no organization, has the funds to restore Santanoni." He paused absently running his hand through his hair.

"There is an encouraging note to all this. The lodge and supporting structures at Newcomb Lake have been reviewed by the State Historical Preservation officer. So have the old farm site and the gatehouse. All three have been declared eligible for inclusion in the National Register of Historic Places. The gatehouse has been selected to become a tourist information center. Thanks to our governor, God bless him, it has been singled out for immediate financing. Keep a close watch on what happens with the other buildings at Santanoni."

He rose, picked up his coffee cup, and took it to the kitchen. "I really must be going, Alyce. Thanks for the coffee."

"You're welcome. You've been a big help." She smiled her thanks and then laughed. "I'll remember you when you're up for reelection."

"If the matter should come to a referendum, and that's entirely possible, you can count on my support." He brushed her check with his warm lips and headed for the door. At that precise moment, the doorbell rang. He turned to Alyce. "Expecting someone?"

Alyce shook her head and opened the door. "Hello, Alyce. I hope you don't mind my dropping in. . ."

Bill Morgan's chin dropped when he saw Alyce was not alone. "I'm sorry, I didn't realize you had company." His tone was relatively civil, but his mahogany eyes were blazing.

"Not at all. I was just leaving." Joe turned to Alyce.

She merely stared, tongue-tied. "I'll be seeing you."

Alyce watched him go down the steps. She had appreciated his coming, but now she was stalling for time. She didn't want to face Bill. The fire in his eyes had not been fueled by brotherly love.

Slowly she turned around. Bill was staring at her trying to draw a response. His dark eyes seemed to probe her very soul. A suffocating sensation tightened her throat. She wanted to explain that Joe was a friend of the family but it was too late now. As uncomfortable as she felt, she was also excited. She dropped her eyes to avoid his stare. "Come in," she said. "I'll get you a cup of coffee." With that she escaped to the kitchen.

six

Alyce leaned against the refrigerator door. What else could happen tonight? She glanced at her reflection in the coffee pot and sighed. If she could have her way, she'd never go back into the living room. She didn't want to face those smoldering eyes.

She shrugged her shoulders and poured two cups of coffee. She didn't want another cup. She knew already she'd be awake half the night but she needed something to do with her hands. She moistened her dry lips, swallowed, and picked up the coffee.

When she returned to the living room, Bill was sprawled on her velour sofa staring at the photo on the television set. It was a family photo of her with Randy and Maria on Rodney's Windrose when Maria was two years old. As she watched, he slowly lifted himself from the sofa, walked over, and picked up the picture. He studied it a few moments. Gently he returned the photo to its place.

He looked up to see Alyce and slowly he advanced toward her. Then a finger under her chin gently tilted her face upward. He traced the smooth line of her jaw and their eyes met tentatively over the coffee.

In place of the anger she had anticipated, she saw compassion in Bill's eyes. She swallowed to relieve the tightness in her throat.

"I brought you a cup of coffee." She gestured toward the sofa. "Please, won't you sit down?" She eased herself onto the sofa and gestured to the cushion beside her. A fleeting smile touched the corners of his mouth.

"I really am glad to see you. . . ." She hoped he couldn't hear her heart hammering in her head.

He seated himself to her right. His slender fingers wrapped around the cup as he lifted it to his lips. She was pleased he was not wearing a wedding band. She hadn't thought about that before.

"How have you been? And how's my friend Max?"

"Oh, we're fine. How have you been? Is your business in Syracuse completed?"

"No, it isn't." He continued. "I stopped to ask if you would have dinner with me tomorrow evening." He studied her face. "But perhaps you have other plans."

Alyce caught the inference and hesitated before responding. She didn't want him to know how eager she was to be with him. "Well," she responded as though she wasn't quite sure she could manage it, "let me check my calendar."

She retrieved her datebook from her purse and studied it carefully. "Yes, I'm free tomorrow evening." She didn't tell him, but if she hadn't been, she would have moved mountains to become so. "What time did you have in mind?"

"Suppose I pick you up about seven. I was afraid you might not be free on such short notice." He glanced at his watch. "I must be going. I have some work to finish tonight. I'll see you tomorrow evening."

At the door Bill turned to face her and his dark thoughtful eyes looked straight into hers. She was unnerved by the tenderness reflected in them and her heart leaped. He dipped his head and Alyce knew then that he was going to kiss her. His mouth caressed her lips lightly. "Good night, Alyce."

As Alyce closed the door, her knees felt like she had climbed Mount Marcy. She unplugged the coffee pot in the kitchen and then gave Max a good night pat and floated into her bedroom.

The next day Alyce had difficulty thinking about her patient but fortunately Mrs. Spellman slept a lot. *What will I wear? Should I try something a bit more sophisticated with my hair than my ponytail? I don't want Bill to think I'm a country bumpkin.*

She shook her head. "Keep your mind on your work," she scolded herself out loud. "You're thirty, not thirteen! This is just a friendly dinner date. Nothing more." But while common sense said one thing, her heart was thumping out a different message.

It was nearly six when she got home from work the next day. She fed Max and let him out for a run in his yard. When she stepped into the shower, she still hadn't decided what to wear. Alyce didn't own many clothes. She wore her uniforms to work and spent her weekends in jeans and pullovers. The only time she dressed up was for church.

She decided on her favorite suit, a gentle Ming plaid with a knife-pleated skirt and a fitted jacket. Though many women had to stay away from pleats, her petite figure made them flattering. The fitted jacket accented her graceful curves and the delicate Irish lace on the collar and cuffs of her matching blouse added just the right touch. Alyce felt good when she wore this suit. Ming green was her color.

She wore her black pumps that matched her leather

clutch bag. Golden hoop earrings and matching twin bracelets completed her ensemble.

Bill arrived a few minutes before seven, but she was ready. He greeted her with a smile that was warm enough almost to make her forget the coat. "I don't believe this. A woman ready on time. Are you for real?"

It was Alyce's turn to laugh. "Yes, indeed. Very real. It goes with my upbringing. My aunt insisted on punctuality."

"Your aunt?"

"Yes. Aunt May. My mother died when I was born. My dad never came back from Europe. He was in the army, a career man. My Uncle Patrick was killed in the same freak accident with my father. So my mother's sister took me in. She had a five-year-old daughter at that time. Aunt May reared the two of us alone. She treated me just like she treated Barbara. We didn't have much money, but we were happy."

Alyce continued her explanation as she got her Harris tweed overcoat from the hall closet. "We had enough money for food and clothing and things like that, but not for luxuries. Aunt May gave us love and understanding in place of the things that money could have bought. I appreciate that now."

The lines of concentration deepened on Bill's brow as he listened to her story. Alyce smiled at the handsomely attired man who had come to take her to dinner. The perfect executive, she thought, as she appraised his impeccable three-piece suit and tastefully patterned tie. Bill opened the door and then a firm masculine arm curved around her waist as he guided her to his car.

A myriad of dangerous thoughts fluttered through

Alyce's mind. Bill's gentle gestures reminded her of Randy. She had loved him with all her heart, but she had ceased wearing her emotional pain like a cement shroud.

"I've made reservations at Sylvia's. I hope that you approve," he said, interrupting her reverie. "I'm sorry I didn't think to ask if you had a favorite restaurant."

"Sylvia's will be fine." Dollar signs flashed before her eyes. She had lived in Syracuse for a number of years but she had never eaten at Sylvia's. Whenever she had occasion to dine out, it was at a more conservative establishment.

The dining room of Sylvia's was ornate, with huge crystal chandeliers and cozy tables spread with snowy white linen. Candles glowed softly from their black wrought-iron holders. Soft dinner music, which Alyce recognized as one of her favorite symphonies from Tchaikovsky, added an elegant but soothing touch.

This was not the atmosphere in which Alyce routinely lived her life, but tonight she felt both comfortable and special. A few female heads looked wistfully at Bill and enviously at her. She ignored the smiles of appreciation that were aimed in her direction.

Alyce appreciated the meticulously dressed waiter with his crisp red bow tie who led them to their table. He exuded efficiency as he filled their water glasses. They had been seated no more than a minute when an attractive cocktail waitress materialized at their side. With her red and white miniskirt uniform, black braid, and black net stockings, she was dressed to please the male diners.

"Good evening. My name is Diane. I'm your cocktail waitress this evening. May I bring you a drink before dinner?"

Alyce declined politely, and so did Bill. Hiding her disappointment behind a painted smile, the waitress excused herself.

Bill looked at Alyce. "Are you a teetotaler?"

Alyce nodded. "I don't need what drinks have to offer. How about you?"

"I wasn't always, but I've become one. I admire people who don't drink and who don't make a big issue about their abstinence."

At that point Philip arrived at their table. He bid them good evening and presented them menus. "I recommend our beef bourguignon this evening," he said. "I'll be back to take your orders once you have had time to make your selections."

Alyce chose chicken Cordon Bleu while Bill opted for a rare prime rib. After their order was taken there was a brief silence as if each were weighing his words before beginning a conversation. Bill smiled at Alyce totally unaware of how he was unsettling her equilibrium with his glance.

The conversation drifted to likes and dislikes in food, clothing, books, and hobbies. In no time at all the waiter returned with their salads and rolls. They were discussing their interests in sports when he arrived with their entrees. A half-hour later, they were still chatting easily.

They had almost finished dinner when a stranger, short and balding, stopped at their table.

"If it isn't Bill . . ."

Before he could finish his greeting, he was interrupted by Bill's enthusiastic response. "Hey! What do you say, Paul?"

"Well, hello, old buddy! How are you? When did you get back to the States? And what are you doing in Syracuse?"

The men shook hands vigorously, the newcomer grinning with pleasure at having discovered an old friend.

"I'm fine, Paul. It sure is great to see you again. I've been home for about a month now." Bill then introduced him to Alyce and they shook hands.

"Well, Bill, I don't want to interrupt. It was nice to see you. Give me a call. I'm living in Syracuse now. Have my own business, and business is pretty good. Look me up, okay? We'll get together for old times' sake. Nice to have met you, Ms. Anderson." He tipped an imaginary hat and rejoined his friends.

Bill glanced at Alyce and realized that she had finished her dinner. Philip headed toward their table.

"Would you like dessert, Alyce?"

"No, thanks. I couldn't possibly eat another bite." She returned his smile.

Bill signaled for the check and signed it. In no time at all they arrived back at Alyce's apartment. Bill guided her to her door with a gentle hand on her back.

"Would you like to come in?"

Bill paused as though the question stymied him. "I'd enjoy that very much, but I'd better say no. I have a busy schedule tomorrow. There's some paper work I must get done tonight."

"I understand. I've had a lovely time. The dinner was delicious."

"I've had a good time too. Could I see you again soon?"

"That would be nice."

The brief conversation brought them to the door. Bill's

fingers traced the delicate line of her chin as he had done in her apartment. Their eyes met in the semidarkness as his fingers curved around the back of her neck and drew her to his chest. He lowered his attention to her softly parted lips. His kiss was gentle. Raising his mouth from hers, he gazed into her eyes. "Good night, Alyce . . . I'll call you."

Alyce watched until the car door slammed behind him. His kiss had sent another stunning reminder of what she had been missing for nine years.

She put her purse on her bed and took off her coat. Then she turned on the light and looked at herself in the mirror. Slowly she touched her lips with her fingers. Not since Randy's death had she been kissed like that.

She wrapped her arms about herself and closed her eyes. Bill had stirred something in her that she had bound up years ago. For years she had existed, even happily at times, without romantic attachments. Now she was struggling against a desire so pure and natural she was unnerved. She hadn't been looking for male companionship, but Bill Morgan had come barging into her life anyway. How she hoped he would stay.

Back at his hotel room Bill removed his tie, kicked off his shoes, and made himself comfortable at his desk. He needed to make some corrections on his manuscript before he met with his editor the next day. He stared at the papers, but his mind refused to focus on the lines needing his attention. He got up, got a drink of water, and tried again. It was no use. He wandered over to the window and looked out at the street lights. He could not get Alyce off his mind.

He thought about their first meeting at Santanoni, and then when he had decided to cultivate her friendship to learn more about his family. Since Will and Nellie were dead, what could she tell him that really mattered? He had no need to continue seeing her, except that he felt drawn to her like a black labrador drawn to water.

What an impression he must have made on her with his bullying questions the first time they met! At first he considered her too feisty, but as he got to know her, he respected her spunk. She had been honest and open with him since the day they met. He wished he had treated her the same way. Though she looked like a fragile china doll, he sensed she would not break easily. He'd hate to oppose her on a matter she felt was important. He knew she would fight for her principles.

Well, Bill . . . the roving bachelor, eh? You could have had any woman you wanted while you floated around Europe. Now you come home to untold disappointment. You fall for a squatter on your land. Correction! Your former land! Sure she's attractive, intelligent, and honest. Are you really ready to settle down? And what about Santanoni? What are you going to do about your old home?

He inhaled deeply and sighed with remorse. He had hoped to see a lawyer while in Syracuse, but thus far his time had been eaten up with his publisher. His mind reeled with his problems, but his heart kept returning to Alyce.

Her responses to his touch and to his kiss told him she found him desirable. But how desirable would he be when she found out he had lied about his name? He shuddered thinking of how close Paul had come to revealing the truth. Maybe it would have been better if he had not interrupted him. That might have given him an opportunity to explain to Alyce. But what explanation could he give for such inane behavior?

A dull ache was spreading across Bill's forehead. He had made a mess of things and he needed to get some sleep. As he turned out the light and eased himself into bed, one thought consumed him. Soon . . . very soon . . . he would tell Alyce.

seven

Alyce had lots of time to think as she drove to Newcomb. Despite her attempts at putting everything in its proper perspective, her thoughts centered on Bill Morgan. What an enigma he had become to her. Something about him was familiar, but she knew she hadn't met him before. Why was he angry when he met her and Max at Santanoni? Why did he ignore her after their pleasant dinner date?

"I'll call you . . . ." His words still echoed in her ears. But he hadn't called. By now he must be back in Newcomb. She wondered what he was doing. She shrugged her shoulders as she parked her Escort in front of the office of Robert D. Roberts.

After Joe Heisler's visit she decided she needed a lawyer to investigate some of Joe's suggestions for saving Santanoni. She could find a lawyer in Syracuse, but since Roberts lived in the Adirondacks, he was more apt to be tuned in to the regulations of the Adirondack Park Agency. Robert Roberts had left no doubt in her mind that he would enjoy helping her. She would try to forget Bill Morgan and get on with saving Santanoni.

The attorney's young secretary greeted her. "Come right in, Ms. Anderson. Mr. Roberts is expecting you." She flashed Alyce a welcoming smile that quieted the butterflies in her stomach momentarily. But it was obvious that she had a consuming interest in what would transpire between Alyce and her boss.

Robert Roberts rose to greet her. "How do you do, Ms. Anderson? I'm glad to see you again." There was an awkward pause. Then he took her hand. "I'm glad I can serve you once more."

"How do you do? I appreciate your arranging our meeting at this hour. I hope it didn't inconvenience you too much."

"Not at all. Do have a seat and we'll get to work." He gestured to a Chippendale chair opposite his oak desk. "I've done some research on the great camps and I've come up with a suggestion. It's an encouraging note that the gatehouse at Santanoni has been selected as a Tourist Information Center. At least the governor is on your side."

Alyce settled back into her chair. She needed the help of more than the governor. She hoped she'd get some workable suggestions from Robert Roberts.

The attorney's steely blue eyes swept over Alyce as he began his explanation. "Here is my suggestion. I believe it will be acceptable to the state legislature, and I think it handles the Adirondack Park Agency's 'Forever Wild' clause in a satisfactory manner. Listen carefully and then tell me what you think about my plan.

"I suggest you form a nonprofit foundation for Santanoni. The members of the foundation would provide the initial funds to begin the restoration of the camp. They would submit a proposal to the state for a management agreement."

Alyce interrupted. "Excuse me, but is a management agreement the same as a lease?"

"No, it isn't. According to the 'Forever Wild' clause, a lease would be unconstitutional. If the legislature accepts your proposal, then it will likely have to come before the voters for their approval."

Alyce nodded. Joe had mentioned a referendum.

Mr. Roberts continued. "We have no way of knowing how the public will vote in a referendum. We can be optimistic though. A few years back the people of New York State voted an overwhelming approval when the fate of Camp Sagamore was in the balance."

He paused again. "You know, Ms. Anderson, it's a strange situation. We feel we know what is best for our own property. Yet the whole state gets to decide what we can do with it. I'm not sure I agree with that policy. What gives me the right to decide what folks anywhere else should do with their public lands?"

Alyce pondered his question. "That's the way it is, isn't it? People who want to come here for a vacation don't want us to do anything to disrupt their fun. They don't see the situation as we do, do they? I wonder how those people would like it if we in the Adirondacks told them how to handle their property in Manhattan or their condominiums in Coral Gables?"

"I hear what you are saying, Ms. Anderson. We have to accept things as they are at the present. I would suggest you find some people who share your interest in the great camp and who are financially able to assist in this project."

"Do you have any idea how much money we'd have to come up with initially?"

"Yes, I do. I'd say you'd need a minimum of $500,000. It will probably take twice that amount to restore Santanoni, but if you have half of the money up front, that would be a good start. If you had a five-member foundation, each would need to give $100,000. If I recall correctly, you have that much from the Hayes estate. If you had another $100,000 of your own, you would have two votes which would give you control over the foundation."

Alyce coughed at the thought of having another $100,000 at her immediate disposal.

"If the foundation came up with $500,000, the funds could be invested immediately so they could draw interest while you await legislative approval. Meanwhile you could advertise your goals and solicit funds from the public."

Alyce settled more comfortably into her chair. Asking Robert Roberts for help seemed to have been a smart move on her part. She listened as he continued his explanation.

"The foundation would have to restore Santanoni at its own expense. Once the restoration was completed and the camp was able to turn a profit, it would be good for public relations to contribute a percentage of that profit to the Adirondack Park Agency, or some other group working to preserve the Adirondack Mountains."

Alyce was forming a plan in her mind. "Of course we would respect the wilderness character of the surrounding Forest Preserve, and we'd be careful to observe the state regulations. We'd continue to restrict access to the camp. Visitors would have to hike into the camp or travel on horseback."

"Good thinking on your part. What you're suggesting would be essential to any proposal you make. Now let's think about the buildings. I'd suggest restoring the lodge first to make it available to those who like to explore the Adirondacks. I mean hikers, skiers, and hunters."

"And fishermen, horseback riders, architectural buffs,

and nature lovers," Alyce added.

The attorney continued. "You might offer tours, light meals, and simple overnight accommodations at reasonable rates. To avoid overuse, you could insist that those coming to Santanoni register in advance."

Alyce had another idea. "Perhaps the foundation could offer a program of nature interpretation to complement what is offered at the interpretative center at the gatehouse."

It was Roberts's turn to smile. "You have some good ideas too. You should be able to find others who care enough to give their financial support to save Santanoni. I believe the state will listen to a foundation that is holding $500,000 in its hands. One of the reasons Santanoni has fallen into such disrepair has been the lack of funds. The state sold Topridge when it couldn't afford to keep it. If we show how we can save Santanoni without disturbing the environment, we should be able to save it too."

Alyce's brow furrowed, but she was encouraged by what the attorney was saying. The bottom line was the financial arrangements. "I don't know four people who know about Santanoni, to say nothing of their being willing to part with that amount of cash to secure its future."

"At the risk of being presumptuous, I have begun to seek out some interested parties for you. I felt if you trusted me as your attorney, you would not object."

"Not at all. I want to carry out the wishes of Will and Nellie Hayes. I'd like to restore Santanoni for them." She was pensive and Roberts hesitated to interrupt her thoughts.

After a brief silence she asked, "Did you find anyone who was interested in the kind of partnership you are suggesting?"

"As a matter of fact I did. I have two prospects." He looked at her directly. "If you would permit me to do so, I would like to become one of the members of the foundation. Not just to prove I think the idea is sound, but because I care about Santanoni too."

Alyce bristled inwardly at his suggestion.

"Though I'm a newcomer to the Adirondacks, relatively speaking, I'm at home in the mountains. After practicing law in Syracuse for five years, I had my fill of city life. I wanted to return to a less populated area. That's one reason why I established my office here in Newcomb."

He went on to explain how he had grown up in the Blue Ridge Mountains of Virginia. "After you came to see me that first time, I hiked in to the Santanoni Preserve. I'm not sure what I was expecting, but I was appalled when I saw that magnificent lodge deteriorating like a long neglected castle. To let that building fall down would be a crime. If it goes, it will take with it a piece of our Adirondack heritage."

As he spoke Alyce could see his deep appreciation for Santanoni. Since he had suggested the criteria for membership in the foundation, he must have the financial resources required. Yet in the back of her mind she remembered their first meeting. Was he offering his help because he was interested in Santanoni? Or was he only interested in her?

"I appreciate your offer, Mr. Roberts. Please give me some time to think about it." *And some way to politely tell you no*, she wanted to add.

"That's fine with me. If you decide to include me in the foundation, you'll need to get another lawyer to handle the establishment of the foundation. If you wish, I could suggest someone. But perhaps you'd rather handle that yourself."

Alyce appreciated his frankness. She pondered his offer, but she would not be hasty in her decision. After a few minutes, her eyes brightened. "You said you had two possibilities? Who is the other?"

"Again at the risk of being presumptuous, I took the liberty of talking with an acquaintance, who, unlike me, is a native of this area. Assuming you would be spending the night at the Antlers, I arranged dinner for the three of us this evening at the inn. Our reservations are for six-thirty."

He studied her face to see if she were angry. Ever so slowly a smile made its way through her mask of uncertainty. Robert Roberts was being helpful; she'd consider his true motives later. Today he had kept his place. She would trust him through dinner.

"My thanks again. Of course I'm staying at the Antlers." She chuckled. It was not only a comfortable inn, it was the only lodging in Newcomb.

At precisely six-thirty Alyce left her room for the dining room. She hadn't had time to think about their afternoon meeting, but she'd consider Roberts's suggestions on her drive back to Syracuse. She was toying with the idea of getting up early so she could hike into Santanoni at dawn. She'd have time to do that and still not be too late getting home if she didn't linger long at the camp. She wished she had brought Max along with her.

As she scanned the dining room for Roberts, a gasp escaped her lips. Sitting with his back to the door, his broad shoulders visible above the chair back, a man was

deep in conversation with her attorney. She strode into
the dining room and came face to face with Bill Morgan.

eight

A tumble of muddled thoughts and feelings assailed Alyce as she tried to force her confused emotions into order. What was Bill Morgan doing here? She took a deep breath but still she could not get her tongue to move. The two men rose to greet her, Robert Roberts exuding his usual charm and Bill with a look of utter astonishment.

For a few moments Bill and Alyce contemplated each other, their bemused eyes locked in silence. The attorney, sensing something was going on to which he was not privy, glanced nervously from one to the other. Unable to comprehend the situation or to endure the silence, he yanked at his tie and asked, "Have you two already met?"

Not trusting herself to speak, Alyce gestured to Bill. Bill turned from Alyce to face Robert Roberts. During that brief moment the puzzlement in his eyes turned to anger. Alyce could not help but recall the way his dark eyes had blazed when they had met at Santanoni, and when he had found Joe Heisler at her apartment.

Alyce watched his lips tighten. A flush of fury darkened his face. She prayed that anger would never again be unleashed against her. She was glad she was neither the cause nor the target of his rage.

"Yes, Rob, Alyce and I have met. I wish you'd not been so secretive about this meeting." He spoke through clenched teeth and there was a chill in his voice as he addressed the lawyer, his words landing like hailstones

on a tin roof. "You could have saved us both some embarrassment."

He turned back to Alyce. "Please sit down, Alyce. I
apologize for what has happened. There are a few details
about this meeting that I had not been told."

Discovering Alyce's direct involvement in the future of
Santanoni had caught Bill off guard. He gave her a sidelong glance and tried to disguise his annoyance at the
revelation, but his vexation was obvious. *Well,* he mused,
Ms. Anderson doesn't reveal the whole truth either. There
was much more he needed to learn about this enigmatic
nurse from Syracuse.

The tense situation was eased momentarily by the waitress coming to take their orders. As she departed for the
kitchen Bill turned again to Alyce.

"Please believe me, I had no idea I would be meeting
you here this evening. I assure you it's a pleasure." He
paused. "I owe you an explanation for not calling before I
left Syracuse, but that's a matter for us to discuss at
another time and place."

Alyce attempted a smile. She would be civil though
she, too, was angry at Roberts. Why didn't he tell her he
had talked with Bill about the foundation plans? Just what
was Bill's interest in Santanoni? She knew so little about
him. Since Robert Roberts had invited him to consider
becoming part of the foundation to save Santanoni, he
must have money. Paupers didn't drive Lincolns.

If only she hadn't allowed herself to become interested
in him. She didn't know how or where it had happened,
but she had to admit she had fallen in love with Bill. In
many ways he was a stranger, but one with very endearing ways. Well, she would let Roberts take charge of this

meeting. He had arranged it. She would listen and try to be rational, but it would be hard with Bill Morgan sitting beside her.

Robert Roberts cleared his throat and fumbled again with his tie. He glanced from Alyce to Bill as he spoke. "Well, I guess I've made a first-class faux pas this time. I apologize to both of you."

Alyce couldn't remain mute all evening. True, he had not handled this situation well, but what was done was done. He couldn't start the evening all over again.

"I forgive you. We all err sometimes." She sounded more magnanimous than she felt.

"That goes for me too." Bill's voice was firm, but it had lost its angry edge.

"I hope I haven't spoiled your dinner. Perhaps we can discuss my proposal after we have eaten."

Before they could answer, the waitress returned with their rolls and salads. Bothered by the unanswered questions that swirled about her, Alyce picked at her food. What interested Bill so much about Santanoni? Robert Roberts had referred to him as a native of the area, but that's all she had learned about him from the attorney.

She knew Bill had been in Europe for several years. He had some kind of business to attend to in Syracuse. He knew how to befriend a dog. He seemed at home in the woods.

The conversation was light as they ate their dinners. Over coffee the attorney cleared his throat to signal the start of the business at hand.

"Ms. Anderson, with your permission, I'd like to tell Bill about my suggestion for a foundation to save

Santanoni." He looked at her, seeking her approval, and she knew he was sincere in asking. Not having any reason to refuse other than the peculiar way he had arranged the dinner meeting, she nodded affirmatively.

Robert Roberts sighed, took a deep breath, and began to explain his plan to Bill. As he made his suggestions, the lines of concentration deepened along Bill's brow and under his eyes.

". . . so I think such a foundation would be acceptable to the Adirondack Park Agency and to the State of New York. I am excited about the possibilities, and I've told Ms. Anderson I'd like to be one of the five members." He glanced at Alyce as he concluded his explanation.

Bill looked at Alyce with questioning eyes before he responded. Though he could see determination and strength reflected in her face, he could not discern her reaction to the possibility of his becoming a part of the foundation. When he spoke, his voice was firm and final.

"Well, Rob, I must say you have done your homework." He turned to Alyce. His voice was calm, his gaze steady. "Since you two have already discussed this plan, I presume you find it acceptable." He spoke in such a way that she could agree or disagree without giving offense.

Alyce nodded her assent. The thought of having Bill as part of the foundation was causing her pulse to race. She'd have to be dead to ignore the excitement that was growing within her as she considered the prospect of having him working by her side to carry out the wishes of Nellie Hayes.

She was glad that Bill was interested in Santanoni, glad that this meeting had been arranged. But could she act rationally with him so close? It wouldn't do to let him know how she felt about him. He had promised to call her but he had broken his promise. Could he be depended on now? The way her heart was pounding, she knew she'd give him another chance.

Finally she gained her voice. "The plan sounds workable to me. I have explained to Mr. Roberts that I do not know others who would be interested in this kind of an investment." She swallowed. "I appreciate the interest both of you have shown in Santanoni. At this point I don't understand why either of you should care so much about the camp, but I'm glad that you do."

She glanced from Bill to Robert Roberts. "Will you please give me time to think about this? I don't make hasty decisions. I need to look for other interested parties should I decide the three of us could work together." She knew she wanted Bill as part of the group. She wasn't so sure about Robert Roberts.

"That's fine with me. It's your ball game." Bill looked at her as if he were analyzing her reaction. "I spent a lot of time at Santanoni when I was a kid. I'd like to help restore the camp to the way I remember it." As he spoke his eyes clouded. He blinked and turned away.

"I agree, Ms. Anderson." Roberts smiled at her. "Do you think a month would be sufficient time for you to make up your mind? We don't mean to rush you, but Santanoni can't wait. The deterioration goes on. If you accept us as partners, remember you'll need to find another lawyer. The sooner you set your plans in motion, the better it will be for the camp."

"I understand that. A month is enough time." She looked at Bill, his expression unreadable. "I'll let you know my decision within thirty days. Thank you for dinner. Now if you will excuse me, I'd like to go to my room." She nodded at both men as they rose from the table.

Alyce felt wrapped in an invisible warmth as she left the dining room. Once in her room she replayed the latest events in her real-life drama. Not in her wildest imaginings did she expect to have dinner with Bill Morgan tonight. She had hoped she might see him again though she had no idea how that would happen.

Her head was so full of new considerations she felt it would burst. There was one place she knew she could go to sort things out: Sunrise would find her hiking into Santanoni Preserve. She didn't understand fully, but she knew God spoke to her most clearly in the out-of-doors. She slipped into her nightgown and settled herself under the homey patchwork quilt, closing her eyes on a world of intriguing possibilities.

The earliest rays of dawn were chasing away the darkness when Alyce signed the camper's register at the gatehouse. She missed Max but this would not be a leisurely hike. She must be on her way back to Syracuse by one o'clock. If she walked briskly, she'd be able to spend an hour at the lodge.

The dry leaves crunched under her feet as she set her face toward Santanoni. She had made it a habit to keep her daypack in the trunk, and today she was glad she had. She knew the importance of taking sufficient water on every hike and she also tucked in an orange she had saved from breakfast.

The chipmunks were still racing through the forest, and at one point she startled a partridge. The poor bird gave a frightened squawk and disappeared into the thicket.

Alyce hiked up the gentle incline that led directly to

Santanoni's impressive lodge and sat down on the steps to see what was going on out on the lake. She wished she had her binoculars.

She had been sitting there for perhaps twenty minutes when she heard someone whistling. Then she heard footsteps on the porch of the lodge around the corner from where she sat. Whoever was coming wasn't trying to be quiet. If Max were with her she'd feel a lot more comfortable about being alone—and vulnerable—five miles into the wilderness.

She got up and headed in the direction of the footsteps. They echoed louder as the intruder walked from one section of the labyrinthine porch toward the place where she had been sitting. She rounded the corner at her usual speedy clip and collided with a familiar six-foot frame.

The collision startled her, but Bill steadied her and then maintained his gentle but firm grip on her arm. Ever so slowly he drew her to his steely chest, and she thrilled to the rippling of his arm muscles as he held her to him. The movement of his breathing sent electrifying vibrations through her as he searched her eyes for an affirmative response. Her heart fluttered wildly in her throat.

"I'm so glad I've found you here," he murmured into her hair. His breath was warm and moist and her heart raced. Instinctively she wound her arms around his neck. Standing on tiptoe, she touched her lips to his. His response was gentle and his lips were warm and sweet.

Aware of his strength and the warmth of his flesh, Alyce felt a tingling in the pit of her stomach. She knew she must disengage herself and so gently she placed her hands on his cheeks and pulled away from him.

"Why did you come looking for me? How did you know

I was here?"

Bill took her by the hand and led her to the steps where they could sit together. "I took a chance, and I'm so glad I did. I have a lot of explaining to do. First, there's the matter of the phone call. I. . ."

Alyce laid a gentle hand over his lips. "Tell me some other time, okay? I have to leave soon. Can we just sit and enjoy this lovely spot together until then?"

Bill nodded. "Fair enough," he said. They sat in silence for a few moments. Then Bill spoke again. "Alyce, will you come back to Santanoni for me? I have commitments that will keep me here for the next six weeks. I can't come to see you. Please come to me."

Alyce did not trust her voice. Bill did care about her. That was all that mattered. Her mind was racing as fast as her heart. At that moment she would have climbed Mt. Marcy in her bare feet if he had asked her to do it for him.

"Will you come back and have Thanksgiving dinner with me? I don't have any family here. It would mean a lot to me. You could stay at the Antlers and we could come back to Santanoni and I could show you around."

Alyce's voice was soft when she responded. "I would enjoy that very much."

His dark eyes glistened. "I promise I won't badger you about your decision concerning the foundation or its members. But if you should decide to count me in, maybe we could begin to make some plans together."

Alyce nodded and then glanced at her watch. "I'm sorry, but I must head back to the gatehouse. Thanks. . .for coming to look for me."

It was Bill's turn to smile. "I assure you, madam, it

was my pleasure. May I walk back with you?"

Alyce flashed him her warmest smile as she took his hand.

nine

Alyce was not able to leave Syracuse as early as she had hoped. It was one-thirty when she finally headed east to Newcomb. Bill wasn't expecting her until the next day so that was no problem. She put a cassette into the player, allowed herself the luxury of a long sigh, and settled back into her seat. The gentle strains of "Liebestraum" would quiet her heart before she had traveled too many miles. She was grateful for a good weather report. She didn't like driving on slippery roads, and New York weather in late November was unpredictable.

Snow had begun to fall in big fluffy flakes when she arrived at the Antlers Inn. "I hope there's a room available tonight," she muttered to herself. "Why didn't I take time to make a reservation? Serves me right if I have to sleep in my car." Suddenly the snow didn't look so lovely.

Fortunately there was one room available. Glancing at her watch, she decided she had better have dinner right away. The Antlers Inn was located in a remote section of the Adirondacks and, consequently, did not draw the kind of clientele that dined fashionably late. She would unpack after she had eaten. She looked forward to a relaxing evening, something that her work schedule of late had not allowed. She pulled the door shut behind her, stuffed her key into her jeans pocket, and headed downstairs.

She chose a table in the rear of the cozy dining room with a good view of the doorway. She enjoyed watching diners come and go. Her waitress was soon at her table to remove the extra place setting. Alyce picked up the menu and scanned it.

She was about to place her order when some other guests arrived for dinner. She glanced toward the entrance and felt her heart race. Coming through the doorway was Bill Morgan looking as handsome as ever in a blue turtleneck and navy trousers. Reluctantly Alyce tore her gaze from his face only to note that clinging to his arm was a gorgeous blond. Not one hair was out of place in her stylish French twist. Her black, long-sleeved dress was simple in design and moved in a fluid motion with her slender body. Despite the woman's natural beauty and style, her countenance was grave, her features drawn.

The color drained from Alyce's face as she stared at the couple. Her stomach slowly tied itself into a hard knot and she had difficulty breathing.

"Ma'am? Are you all right? Excuse me, ma'am, are you okay?" The young waitress put a gentle hand on Alyce's shoulder.

The concern on the young woman's face was the catalyst Alyce needed to cushion her shock. She shuddered. "I'm so sorry to have frightened you. I'm okay. Just tired, I guess." She tried to smile to put the waitress at ease.

"I'll have a tuna on rye, toasted, please, and a cup of black coffee." Alyce hated tuna fish, and she didn't like coffee at night, but that was the first thing that came to mind. She didn't want the waitress hovering over her.

As she gazed at Bill's companion, she had a sneaking suspicion that that woman, whoever she was, would look

regal in a potato sack. It was time she reexamined her
relationship with Bill Morgan. Was she interested in him
only as a member of the Foundation to Save Santanoni?
It was easy to say that. Before she succumbed to another
tender moment with him, Alyce decided she should know
what she wanted, from him and for herself. She should
also make sure that they shared the same spiritual foundation; she had allowed her emotions free rein for too
long.

Alyce's frenzied thoughts were interrupted by the waitress returning with her sandwich. "May I get you anything else, ma'am?"

Alyce shook her head and the waitress disappeared into
the kitchen. She stared at the sandwich and then made a
half-hearted attempt to eat it but gave up after two tries.
It tasted like fishy cardboard.

"Please, Lord, don't let Bill see me here," she prayed
with her eyes open.

She glanced down, suddenly appalled at her attire.
Faded corduroy jeans, her favorite flannel shirt, and her
old Nikes were far from haute couture. She had intended
to change for dinner when she arrived at the inn. What a
day this had turned out to be. The sooner this day was
over, the better, she surmised, but first she had to decide
what she was going to do about tomorrow.

She swallowed a few sips of her coffee and requested
her check. Her scarcely touched sandwich did not go
unnoticed.

"I'm so sorry you didn't enjoy your sandwich. Was
there something wrong with it?"

"Oh, no," Alyce responded through a pasted-on smile.
"I guess I just wasn't hungry. But I'll make up for it at

dinner tomorrow."

"Great! You'll love our Thanksgiving feast. My name is Babs. I'm working this entire weekend, so I'll see you at breakfast." She looked at Alyce to make certain she was all right. "I hope you rest well."

One glance at Bill assured her he was giving his friend 110 percent of his attention. Not wanting Babs to feel she was at fault for the uneaten sandwich, Alyce left a generous tip. Now for her escape. She tiptoed to the door. Two more steps and she would be out of sight and into the hallway.

Her heart thumped like a metronome gone berserk. For some insane reason she turned around. As she did, Bill looked away from his stunning companion and straight at her. She knew she should flee the dining room, but her sneakers felt nailed to the floor.

Bill turned back to his companion and said something. Then he rose and came toward her. He greeted her with a quick, warm embrace.

"Alyce, I wasn't expecting you until tomorrow. When did you arrive?"

Alyce tried to stay calm. It was obvious he hadn't been expecting her. She glanced at Bill and then at his companion.

"Hello, Bill." Her voice was weak and uncontrolled. She hoped he couldn't see how close she was to tears. "I arrived a short time ago. I left Syracuse later than I had planned." She was mumbling as she edged toward the exit.

Bill put a staying hand on her arm as he sensed she was leaving. "Please, don't go. There's someone I want you to meet." He gently propelled her toward his table.

Short of creating an ugly scene, she could do nothing but accept his invitation to meet his friend. She thought of thirty-nine places she would rather be at that very moment.

Bill made the formal introductions. "I'd like you to meet my sister, Bette Montgomery."

Alyce retrieved her false smile and pasted it on again. "How do you do, Bette? I'm pleased to meet you." She hoped she sounded sincere. She wondered how much longer her legs would hold her up.

Bette extended her hand. It was a friendly gesture on her part, but something was clearly awry. Alyce's nursing instincts detected tension in her grasp.

"Won't you join us for a cup of coffee?" It was Bill's invitation.

Alyce hesitated, but Bill pulled a chair out for her anyway.

"This is my lucky day. I don't deserve having the two most beautiful women in the world sitting at my table." Bill beamed his disarming smile, first at Alyce, and then at his sister. "What a great Thanksgiving celebration this is going to be!"

Alyce toyed with her napkin. She was having trouble finding her tongue. She'd better find it soon before Bill's sister decided she was incapable of rational speech. Bette spoke again.

"Bill has told me all about you. I was looking forward to meeting you tomorrow at dinner." Her voice was soft and controlled. "I'm glad you arrived safely."

Feeling like one of Cinderella's stepsisters, Alyce smiled weakly. She was tired, and now she felt chagrin at the false conclusions she had drawn about Bill. She was also more puzzled about Bill's past.

"Thank you, but I'd rather forget the coffee. It's been a traumatic day. I'm sure you'll find my company more acceptable after I've had a good night's rest. I'll see you at dinner tomorrow."

As she delivered her speech, Alyce tried to get used to the idea that Bill had a sister. What other secrets was he harboring?

At this point she didn't know and she was too tired to care. She looked at Bill and then at Bette. "Please excuse me. It was nice meeting you, Bette." She gave Bill a lingering, enigmatic look and left the dining room.

ten

Bill studied his coffee cup after Alyce left their table. Bette watched him for a few moments before she spoke. "You're in love with her, aren't you?"

Bill nodded. "Yes," he said, "but there are complications in our relationship."

Bette smiled knowingly. Her own ill-fated marriage had been destined for disaster. At sixteen she had eloped with her high school art teacher.

"Do you want to talk about them?" She and Bill had shared their troubles when they were growing up. Maybe they could recapture some of that warmth that had bound them together when they had quarreled with their parents.

Bill nodded again and sighed. "Let's go back to your room." He hoped he could find the right words when he got there. Once ensconced in her comfortable quarters, Bette wasted no time.

"Okay, big brother, do you want to tell me what's wrong?"

Bill smiled. It was ironic that Bette was taking the lead in the conversation. "I didn't tell her I had a sister, Bette."

"So? What does that matter? It's obvious she's interested in you. Why else would she come to Newcomb for

Thanksgiving dinner? There certainly are more interesting places to enjoy a holiday."

"It's not just about you. There's something else I haven't told Alyce. Something important." Bill shut his eyes momentarily as if by doing so he could shut out his problems. "Alyce is more than a passing fancy. I'd like to marry her."

"Have you asked her to marry you?"

"No. . . ."

"Come on, Bill. Why not? You've always gone after whatever you wanted."

Bill knew she was alluding to the quarrel that had erupted between him and their father when Bill left for college. He never saw his father again. Bill was wiser now. His problem had been the impatience of youth while his father's had been grief at the disappearance of his younger son.

Bill grinned at his sister. "I haven't changed. But things get so complicated. You see, Alyce is interested in Santanoni."

"So? Why is that a problem? Aren't you interested in our home anymore?"

Bill gulped at her comment. "Of course I am. That's what brought me back from Europe. I wanted to settle down, to spend my time writing. I've got enough ideas to keep me writing for the rest of my life. I came home to reconcile my differences with Will and Nellie. I'd hoped to find you again, and then I looked forward to spending my days writing at Santanoni."

"What's stopping you?"

Bill felt his heart leap into his throat as Bette eyed him carefully. He turned to face her, glad that she was sitting down. She looked so pale. He didn't know where to begin. He couldn't keep his voice from trembling. Growing up at Santanoni, the two of them had been inseparable; Bill had grown to realize only recently how much he loved her. It must have broken her heart to be left behind when he left for college. Now he had to tell her about their parents.

"Bette," he said gently, "Will and Nellie are dead. They died in Syracuse a couple of years ago."

As painful and difficult as it was for them both, Bill continued. He wasn't sure he'd be able to begin again if he stopped. "After we left home, they sold Santanoni. It now belongs to the State of New York, as part of the Adirondack Park."

When he mentioned the sale of the property, Bette gasped. Though she regretted her estrangement from her parents, she accepted their deaths as inevitable. But to lose Santanoni was too much. During the years since her marriage ended she had become a fashion designer, and a good one too. Along with her talent, she had developed an unshakable professional exterior even when she was being torn to shreds inside. She could usually hide her feelings, but now she trembled like a leaf in a March wind.

Bill continued. "Except for a few minor donations here and there, the bulk of Will and Nellie's estate was bequeathed to the nurse who took care of them during their final years. She's supposed to find a way to restore the camp."

Bette detected a dramatic change in Bill's tone when he mentioned the nurse who was named the beneficiary of the estate.

"The nurse is trying to establish a foundation to save Santanoni," he continued. "I feel so bad that I came back from Europe too late to make peace with Will and Nellie. Why can't we see things more clearly when we are young? We could avoid so much heartache."

Bette did not answer Bill's rhetorical question. She had come home to rest at Santanoni—the doctor had ordered it—and now the one stable thing she had counted on, her old home in the woods, had been yanked away during her absence. She said nothing as she stared into Bill's eyes.

Bill was frightened. Why couldn't he have found a better way to tell her? But even as he chided himself, he knew there was no easy way. Bette was here. She needed to know the truth. *Dear God,* he prayed silently, *don't let the pain be more than she can bear. She's all the family I have left.*

"Bette, are you okay?" He knelt beside her and grasped her hands. At first she said nothing. He took his handkerchief and wiped the tiny rivulets trailing down her cheeks.

Bette's shoulders began to shake as she gave way to sobbing. "I'm too late, Bill. . . ." Her mascara was now streaked across her once lovely face. "Too late . . . too late. God knows I loved Will and Nellie, but they didn't know it." She looked at her brother. "Oh, Bill, I'm too late."

Bill held her until her sobs subsided. He searched for words to comfort her. It was too late for them to mend the relationship with their parents. But they were young, and Santanoni was still there. They could do something about the home they had loved and had lost.

"We'll find a way to save the camp. Perhaps we could become part of the Foundation to Save Santanoni."

Bette looked at her brother and a tentative smile threatened to ease concern on her face. Once they had done everything together. Maybe they could make up for the years they had been separated.

The two sat immersed in their private thoughts for some time. Then Bette remembered they had been talking about Bill's relationship with Alyce. She hoped he'd find a wife and have a happy marriage.

She had arrived only a few hours earlier. They had twenty years of catching up to do. Bill told her where he'd been, about his travels throughout Europe, and about his writing career. He explained that his latest manuscript was in his publisher's hands in Syracuse. He talked about his return to Newcomb.

Then he told Bette about his trip to Santanoni when he discovered backpackers camping in the preserve. "I met Nellie's beneficiary camping on the lake shore," he said. When he mentioned the beneficiary, his tone softened.

After he finished his monologue, Bette had many questions and Bill answered each as best he could. When she probed deeper about the beneficiary, however, he began to choose his words carefully.

Bette was angry that some gold-digging nurse would

be named in her parents' will. She knew she and Bill
were undeserving, but to leave it all to a stranger? She
wanted to know more about this woman.

"What's this nurse like?"

Bill inhaled deeply before replying. "Well, she's a
woodswoman. She loves backpacking and camping. She
comes up to Santanoni from Syracuse a couple of weekends each year with Max."

"Who's Max? Her husband?" She hoped her brother
hadn't fallen in love with another man's wife. He certainly sounded interested in her.

Bill chuckled at her question. "Max is her boxer dog!"

Bette laughed at that. Then she grew silent. "Bill?"
Her tone jerked him to attention. "Is my hideaway still
there?"

Bill smiled in relief. For once he could give an answer
that wouldn't upset her.

"Yes, Bette. The studio is still there guarding your
section of the lake."

He waited a few minutes for Bette to come back to
him. Then he went on. "Well, since I've told you this
much, I might as well confess the rest of it. I seem to
have backed myself into a corner." He swallowed and
then continued. Maybe he'd feel better after he told her.
Perhaps she could help him out of his dilemma.

"When I first met Alyce, I didn't tell her my name."

"What difference does that make?"

"It makes a big difference. I mean I didn't tell her my
real name."

"Come on, Bill. Who did you say you were? Paul

Newman?"

"Bette, it's not funny. I told her my name was William Morgan."

Bette rolled her eyes heavenward. "I'm afraid I don't understand your problem. I thought that was your name!"

Bill was becoming annoyed with Bette. He was in no mood for jokes. He'd try once more to explain. They were both tired and this day had had a full measure of emotional shocks. "She thinks my name is William Morgan. She doesn't know I'm William Morgan Hayes."

Bill could see that Bette didn't consider that a major problem. He went on. "I don't know why I said my name was Bill Morgan. I certainly didn't expect to see her again so it didn't matter who I said I was. I never dreamed I would fall in love with her."

Bette's big blue eyes bored through him like an auger digging post holes. She was beginning to get the picture, but it wasn't quite in focus. She couldn't believe her brother had lied about his name, but that was his problem. Now he was telling her he was in love with two women.

"Let me sort this out, Bill." Bette began to pace back and forth as she eyed him squarely. She could see that he had more than a passing interest in Alyce Anderson. "I find it hard to believe that you deliberately lied about your name. You'd better get that straightened out fast! But take it from me, you're going to get into big trouble courting two women at the same time."

It was Bill's turn to be surprised. "Two women? I have enough complications with one."

Bette's brow furrowed. "Tell me, who do you love? That gold-digging nurse or Alyce Anderson?"

Bill looked at her bemused. Suddenly it all made sense. He threw back his head and roared with laughter. "Bette," he said, as he tried to gain control of himself, "don't make my life more complicated than it already is. Your 'gold-digging' nurse is Alyce Anderson."

eleven

The Thanksgiving dinner at the Antlers Inn was a traditional one served family style. Some of the guests had elected to dress up, while others donned more casual garb. Bill wore his well-cut navy suit. Bette was attired in one of her own creations, a dark brown cashmere dress with a sweetheart neckline. Alyce wore her azure blue dress with the pleated skirt and the long fitted bodice. Her tiny waist was encircled in a filagreed gold belt with tiny tassels.

Bill's eyes sparkled as she approached the dinner table. The three were soon so deep into conversation that they were scarcely aware of the festive food. Bill listened intently as Bette and Alyce got acquainted. All too soon they were finishing their after-dinner coffee.

The conversation had been light and pleasant. Bette turned to Alyce and asked, "Wouldn't it be fun to hike into Santanoni tomorrow morning? The snow isn't too deep. What do you say?"

Alyce liked that idea. "I've never been to Santanoni when there was snow on the ground. That sounds like fun. What you do think, Bill?" As she posed the question, her pulse began to flutter. Although she gave Bette an encouraging smile, inside she wished the two of them could make the trip without Bette.

Alyce's wish was not to be granted. The next morning the three of them enjoyed an early breakfast and arrived at the camp by nine.

"I'll sign us in," said Alyce as she headed for the registration box. Despite the stubby pencil, which like all trailhead pencils needed sharpening, Alyce's handwriting was delicate and precise. She closed the log book and glanced at Bette and Bill. Bette was frowning. Then Bill spoke softly to her and she looked at him and nodded. With Bill in the lead the three of them headed down the snow-covered trail toward the old lodge.

At first sight of the main grounds, Bette uttered a moan. The light snowfall did not hide the overgrown lawn, rotted out buildings, or broken windows. She hastened to the old lodge and peered inside. A steady drip was falling on the buckled hardwood floors as snow melted through the roof.

"Would you like to go inside?" Bill asked as he extricated a key from his pocket.

Alyce's eyebrows shot upward. "Where did you get a key?"

There was a slight hesitation before Bill answered. "You know how it is. You just have to know the right people." He tried to laugh the matter off, but Alyce wasn't smiling. Bill fumbled for a better explanation. "Remember, I grew up around here. I know someone who has a key."

Alyce's brow furrowed as if to question Bill's answer but she trooped obediently into the lodge behind Bette.

Despite the years of neglect, the interior of the first floor was amazingly well preserved and the paneled hallway going up to the second story was in perfect condition. The gigantic stone fireplace stood like a lovely monolith dividing the living room from the dining room. Looking out the front windows, they could see the silent lake, and beyond it, the majestic snow-capped mountain.

Alyce was awed by her surroundings. She couldn't believe she was actually inside the lodge. As she turned to express her thanks to Bill, she noticed Bette gently rubbing her hand over the windowsill, almost like a caress.

After they had explored the main lodge, they headed down to the studio on the shore of Lake Newcomb. Part of the roof had caved in and some windows had been boarded up. When she saw the broken cathedral window, Bette burst into tears.

Bill put his arm around her and drew her close as they walked back to the main lodge and then down to the boathouse. They spent about an hour checking the various states of decay of other buildings. By now the sun had disappeared. Bill suggested it might be wise to head back to Newcomb. "We could be in for some foul weather. Since none of us is dressed for that, we'd better start back."

Though they agreed with him, Bette seemed reluctant to leave. Alyce noticed how often she and Bill had made comments about certain buildings, trees, and even the beach. They seemed very knowledgeable about Santanoni.

They exchanged few words on the hike back to the parking lot. The visit to the great camp had left them in a somber mood. When they reached their car, Bill spoke first.

"It's been a long time since breakfast. Let's go back and get something to eat."

As they drove back to the Antlers, Alyce mentally replayed their outing at Santanoni. Robert Roberts had told her Bill was a native of the area so he and Bette would know about the camp. But Bette seemed interested in every nook and cranny of the lodge. She had lingered long after the others were ready to leave. Why was she so upset when they visited the studio?

Furthermore Bill seemed to be paying more attention to his sister than to her. Alyce might as well stop thinking about the attraction she felt for him and get on with saving Santanoni. At least she would give it her best shot.

The three talked about Santanoni over their late lunch. Alyce commented with a sigh, "It's really a shame to see such a beautiful estate falling apart. Every time I go there, I consider how it could be fixed up if one had unlimited resources."

She paused. "I wish I could find a couple of people who were interested in joining our Foundation to Save Santanoni." She looked at Bill who had just exchanged a furtive glance with Bette.

"I haven't told you, Bill, but I accept your offer to become a part of that group." Alyce hesitated, watching his reaction. Seeing his pleasure at her announcement, she continued. "I'm not comfortable working with Robert Roberts though. I'm sorry. I know he's your friend, but I feel uneasy around him."

Again she looked at Bill to gauge his response. "Do you suppose we could find a lawyer in Syracuse to handle this foundation idea? I know we'd need to find three others to work with us, and maybe that's asking for the impossible." She hoped she hadn't offended Bill, but she felt the need for complete honesty. As she spoke Bette nudged Bill with her elbow.

An awkward silence followed and then Bill cleared his throat. "I have a friend in Syracuse named Peter Brown who specializes in estates. He's part of a team of lawyers. They're former classmates of mine. If you wish, I could ask him to look into this matter for you."

He spoke hesitantly as he looked at Alyce. "Perhaps you should meet Peter and see what legal advice he has to offer."

Bette smiled at Bill's suggestion, but he was waiting for Alyce's response.

"I'd be grateful if you would do that. It's hard for me to know where to turn in legal matters." Randy had always taken care of those things. She thought of how efficient he had been, a trait she admired in a man.

Alyce turned to Bette and Bill. "You know, the Hayeses had a son and a daughter. I wonder what happened to them. They would be so sad to see Santanoni now." She looked down at her hands and then went on. "Well, maybe they wouldn't care. They didn't care much about their parents."

As Alyce voiced her speculations, Bette's eyes brimmed with tears and her lips trembled. Bill diverted Alyce's attention away from her.

"You know the saying, 'Where there's a will, there's a way.' I've always found that to be true. Do you want me to talk with Roberts? I can explain the situation to him in an inoffensive way. He's embarrassed about this whole matter anyway."

"Thank you, Bill, I'd appreciate that." Alyce felt relieved to have that matter settled. She hadn't figured out how to tell the attorney herself, and now she wouldn't have to. *Thank You, Lord. Again You've answered before I asked,* she prayed silently.

"Consider it done," said Bill with an air of efficiency.

Bette had remained silent during this discussion, but when Bill spoke her eyes widened and a warning cloud settled over her features. She opened her mouth as if to comment, but Bill was not finished.

"Bette and I spent a lot of time at Santanoni when we were kids. We know the grounds well."

Alyce stared at him. Why was he telling her this now? Was it because she had told him she wanted him to be a part of the Foundation to Save Santanoni? What else did he know that he hadn't revealed? She made a herculean effort to keep her voice from reflecting her inner turmoil.

Without emotion she asked, "And did you know the Hayeses?"

Sensing the drama that was unfolding, Bette put a gentle but shaky hand on Alyce's arm. Before Bill could respond, she said softly, "Yes, Alyce, we knew them well." She glanced at her brother. "I'm surprised Bill hasn't told you that. So much has happened since we left the Newcomb area. It's been nearly twenty years since we have seen each other. We're both dealing with some weighty emotional trauma."

Looking directly into Alyce's eyes, Bette asked, "Will you let me be the third member of your team to save Santanoni? The camp is the one tie I have with my child-hood. I don't want to let it slip away like so many other things."

Visions of the well-dressed princess paraded before Alyce's eyes. Bette's clothes reflected good taste and financial resources and Bette herself was obviously interested in the camp. If Alyce accepted Bette's offer, she'd need to find only two more benefactors for Santanoni. She smiled at Bette.

"I will give that some thought. Thanks for offering."

Bette nodded as Alyce folded her napkin and left the table.

Alyce had to return to Syracuse Sunday afternoon. The three of them attended worship services at the little village chapel in the morning and then had dinner together at the Antlers. That morning before church the question of Bill's faith had again surfaced in Alyce's mind. Although she and Bill would need to share their Christian testimony in greater depth, she had sensed a sincere desire in Bill as he listened intently to the minister's sermon and held her hand during the congregational prayer.

After four days together Bette and Alyce had become friends. Still the only part of her life that Bette had shared centered on her activities as one of California's hardest working fashion designers.

"Living on the edge of physical and mental exhaustion hasn't been fun," Bette admitted, "but in a way I'm glad. If I hadn't worked myself into such a state, I would never have come home. My doctor insisted I take six weeks off and do nothing. 'Forget Fashion World and your boutiques for a while,' he commanded. At first I ignored him. Then through a strange series of coincidences I found out my brother was coming home from Europe. I sent him a message through some former friends still living in Newcomb. Bill responded by asking me to meet him here at Santanoni."

She looked at Bill. "I'm sorry that I didn't answer the letter you wrote me several years ago. I was glad to hear from you. I guess it shows how much I needed a rest. Last Monday I knew I had to come back here. I was fortunate to get a plane reservation to Albany on such short notice. Someone's cancellation became my blessing." She looked at Alyce. "I'm glad I decided to come home."

"I'm glad you did, too, Bette." Then she added as though it were an afterthought, "I was quite surprised to learn Bill had a sister." She paused looking at Bill. "Your brother will never be accused of talking too much."

With a furtive glance Bette telephoned an urgent message to Bill. For the sake of his future relationship with Alyce, she hoped he wouldn't ignore it.

Bill began to speak, but it wasn't the confession Bette hoped he'd make. "This time I do have something to say. I plan to come to Syracuse the middle of next month. My publisher expects the press sheets for my new book to be run by then." He addressed Alyce. "May I call you when I get there?"

His question reminded both of them of another time when he had promised to call, and Alyce winced at the memory. *So he's a writer,* Alyce mused. *I never suspected that. I was beginning to think he was involved in some sort of undercover work.*

"May I, Alyce?"

She tried to remember his question. Oh, yes. He was coming to Syracuse again and he wanted to call her. She was glad he didn't know how disappointed she was when he didn't call that first time. She had kept her heartache a secret.

"I'll be glad to hear from you when you come to Syracuse, Bill." *Please do call me this time.* She turned to Bette. "Can you come too?"

"We'll see. I'm supposed to be here to rest." She cast a knowing glance at her brother. "Maybe Bill has secrets to share with you. I fear I've been as useful as a toothache this weekend."

"Don't feel that way. Please come if you can." She turned to Bill. "Do you think you'll have time to look up Peter Brown while you're in Syracuse? It would be easier for me if the business of saving Santanoni could be carried out in Syracuse rather than in Newcomb."

"Consider it done but I don't intend this trip to be all business. After I see my publisher, we could go out to dinner and then to the Ice Follies. How does that sound?"

Alyce's eyes brightened. Skating had been one of her favorite winter diversions but she had little time for it anymore. "That sounds lovely."

She looked at her wristwatch and gathered her purse and coat. After giving Bette an affectionate embrace she said, "Take care, Bette, and please come to Syracuse with Bill."

"Perhaps," said Bette. "Drive carefully."

Bill carried Alyce's bag to the car and placed it in the trunk. Then he drew her to him. "Thank you for coming," he whispered, his voice almost lost in her hair. "You don't know how much this meant to me. One day I'll have a lot of explanations for you." He lowered his head and kissed her with lips soft and gentle as the snowflakes that were beginning to fall.

Alyce wound her arms around the warm chest inside his jacket. She could hear his heart beating as they embraced. She would have stayed there forever, but the falling snow brought her back to reality. "I've had a wonderful time," she said as she released her lips from his.

"I'll see you soon, Alyce."

Bill opened her door and she slid in. As he watched her back out of the parking lot and head west, he knew he could not live without her. He would never be content until he had asked her to marry him. Not even another blizzard like the one in '77 would keep him from seeing her in December in Syracuse.

Alyce was thankful the snowfall was light as she drove home. She wanted to think about her weekend with Bill, and she couldn't do that if the driving were hazardous.

The time they had spent together had made her painfully aware of how lonely she was. She could handle the days. But how nice it would be to have someone to love and to come home to each night.

Visions of Bill invaded her thoughts. She remembered every detail of his clothing. No matter what he wore, it enhanced his near perfect physique. She wondered what it would be like to be held in his arms every night. For the first time—without feeling the least bit disloyal to Randy and Maria—she pondered a future with a new husband.

twelve

Bill lost no time in contacting Peter Brown once he had
settled his business with his publisher. Peter's specialty
was legacies, state-owned properties, and the like. He
agreed to contact the Adirondack Park Agency to discuss
the tentative plans that had been made for the Foundation to Save Santanoni. Then he suggested Bill contact
the legal offices of Barkley, Cole, and Murray.

His stint as administrative assistant to a U.S. Senator
gained Bill a listening ear from a team of attorneys whose
expertise could move mountains. It wouldn't hurt the
cause of Santanoni that these men had connections in the
governor's mansion.

Bill deplored using friends to accomplish personal
goals, but with Santanoni at stake, he'd draw on whatever resources he needed. Barkley, Cole, and Murray were
located in downtown Syracuse, not far from the company
that was publishing his book.

Bill left the law office with a spring in his step and his
fingers crossed. Now for a call to one lovely lady. He
had something on his mind to share with Alyce and it
was not just his success at the law office. But first he
must settle the matter he had been avoiding for too long.
He must tell Alyce his full name.

When Alyce arrived home from work, there was a letter in her mailbox. Eagerly she tore open the envelope.

Dear Alyce,

*I'm so sorry I missed you. Our meeting
with Peter Brown is set for next Friday
morning at nine a.m. I'll call you tonight
for confirmation.*

*Love,
Bill*

Alyce grinned. Bill hadn't wasted any time. She had
kept a light work schedule so she could concentrate on
Santanoni. However, when a nursing friend came down
with a serious virus, she agreed to work in her place for
three nights. Now she was sorry, but she always kept her
promises.

Bill called around seven and explained where the law
office was located. He wouldn't be coming to Syracuse
until late Thursday. He would meet her at the attorney's
office Friday morning. His call was brief and business-
like, and Alyce was dismayed by his impersonal tone.

To Alyce the days crept by like a snail in reverse. Friday finally arrived and Alyce arrived a few minutes early
at the law office. The receptionist, a chic, middle-aged
woman, smiled as she gave her name. "Go right in, Ms.
Anderson. Everyone else has arrived." The warm smile
she flashed at Alyce failed to quiet the butterfly ballet in
her stomach. Being with Bill and saving Santanoni was
too much at one time.

The men rose as Alyce walked into the inner office.
Bill's broad smile set her heart racing even faster. Bette
hugged her. After he introduced her to Peter Brown, Bill

motioned for her to sit at his right. She felt like she'd just stepped off a roller coaster.

Peter took charge of the conversation. "Now that we're all here, let's get right to work. I have given your project top priority since Bill contacted me. Both Bill and I have had consultations with Barkley, Cole, and Murray. Your suggestion for the Foundation to Save Santanoni seems to be a viable one. We think the foundation idea will be acceptable to the New York State legislature, and it does not seem to go against the 'Forever Wild' policy of the Adirondack Park Agency."

Alyce relaxed a bit. She liked the way Peter spoke with authority; gratefulness surged through her as she considered Bill's role in securing his help with the Santanoni project.

"I've drawn up copies of the proposal for each of you." He paused to distribute them. "Look carefully at the fine points. See if I have interpreted your wishes accurately. After you have read the proposal, we'll discuss each point." He sat down to await their responses.

Alyce scanned her copy and then went back to the beginning to read it carefully. Legalese was hard for her to interpret and the phrasing intimidated her. The proposal seemed sound to her, however, and it was drawn up according to the suggestions made by Robert D. Roberts.

When everyone had finished reading, Peter Brown answered questions and clarified points. Alyce then raised the issue of two more members for the foundation.

"At this time," she said, "I don't have any possibilities. I'll have to beat the bushes looking for them. I'll do that now that our proposal appears acceptable."

Peter spoke again. "I've taken quite a personal interest

in this effort to save Camp Santanoni. After Bill explained the situation to me, I drove up to Newcomb. Bill took me into the preserve. I experienced the same gut-wrenching feelings as you when I saw what was happening to that magnificent lodge. I'd like to join your foundation, but it would be unethical to handle the legalities and be part of the group too. I'll content myself with helping save Santanoni by being your attorney."

No one commented so he began again. "It's important to move quickly. Surmising that you might not know where to find two other members for your foundation, I took the liberty of making some inquiries. I have two business associates who are interested in joining your Foundation to Save Santanoni. May I suggest Roger Murray and Charlie Cole of Barkley, Cole, and Murray?

"Roger is familiar with the Santanoni Preserve, and he has the legal expertise to find solutions to whatever problems we may encounter. Charlie is an outdoorsman and a preservationist. He loves the Adirondacks and spends as much time up there as he can."

Bill and Bette deferred to Alyce. She looked from one to the other. "I'm willing to accept them on your recommendation if it's okay with Bette and Bill." They nodded affirmatively. Alyce was relieved.

Having settled the important matter of personnel, and seeing nothing wrong with the basic tenets of the proposal, Bill suggested they take the weekend to think about the whole matter.

Peter stood up and offered his hand to all. "I would be pleased if we could do that and meet Monday to sign the papers. I'll contact Roger and Charlie. I'm leaving a week from today for a vacation in the Bahamas. It would be good if we had this proposition ready to submit before I depart."

As they left the law office, Bill suggested the three meet for dinner that evening. "We need to talk about Santanoni. Why not do it over a delicious meal?"

"Oh, Bill, I can't," Bette spoke first. "I've already made some plans to have dinner with the manager of Giselle's Boutique."

Bill looked at Alyce.

"I can't make it either, Bill. I'm covering for a sick friend."

"How about tomorrow then? Could we eat early so we have time to talk? Then we could get tickets to the Ice Follies."

"I'm really sorry, but I've promised to work the next three nights for Peggy."

Bill would not give up. "Then when can we get together? It's important that we discuss this proposal before we sign the papers." He knew it was also important that he discuss something else with Alyce before Monday.

"How about Sunday? We could go to church and then you could come to my apartment for brunch."

Bill and Bette exchanged glances. Although Bill had committed his life to Jesus Christ in recent years, he wasn't sure about Bette. Growing up they were not accustomed to attending church services, except perhaps on holidays. Bill was quite sure that the Thanksgiving Sunday they had gone to church with Alyce was the first time in many years that Bette had entered a church for worship. He didn't want to coerce Bette; still there was no time like the present to be a Christian witness.

"Why not?" It was Bill who had asked the question. "What time shall we pick you up?"

Alyce drove home, gave Max a bit of attention, and had a nap. She would be working from eleven to seven. When she had that shift, she napped a few hours so she would arrive fresh at her patient's home. She'd enjoy thinking about Bill and the future of Santanoni as she took care of Peggy's patient. The one advantage of night shifts was that often the patient slept and she had to do nothing more than be there.

Following the morning worship at Alyce's church, a brunch of fruit, rolls, and cheese was both attractive and tasty. Alyce reflected that the minister's sermon topic, based on the grace of God as reflected by the gift of His Son, was no more a coincidence than her first encounter with Bill Morgan. She was sure both were destined by God.

They ate leisurely as they discussed the Foundation to Save Santanoni. Alyce gazed often at Bill. There was so much she admired about him in both his personality and his appearance. The flip side she determined was that he didn't seem interested in a permanent relationship.

As he discussed Santanoni, Alyce studied his face. It was animated as always when he talked about the camp, but today he seemed distracted. He had something on his mind that he wasn't sharing. She wished they could be alone but the afternoon passed quickly and Bill and Bette left about five.

Maybe she was reading more into their relationship than she should. She hated the thought that Bill might feel Santanoni was more important than her. Things should never take priority over people. She'd have her nap, take care of her patient, and see Bill and Bette at the lawyer's office in the morning.

Bill and Bette had agreed to meet Alyce in the front lobby of the attorney's building at a little before nine. Alyce arrived first, her petite figure encased in a black wool coat. A kelly green scarf about her neck matched her beret and gloves. She stamped the snow from her leather boots. It had been snowing since the previous evening and high boots were in order.

A taxi arrived shortly and deposited a glamorous Bette, clad in a dark brown mink with matching hat. Alyce's heart did a triple beat when Bill appeared from nowhere. The gray lamb's wool collar of his coat complemented nicely his dark hair with its hint of silvery temple "wings." She wondered if he had any idea how his presence excited her. Bette and Bill spotted Alyce at the same time. They smiled and walked over to join her.

"Hi, Alyce. You look stunning. That green does wonderful things for your eyes."

"Thanks, Bette. You look quite elegant yourself."

Bill paused a moment before asking, with a twinkle in his eye, "And what about me?"

"You look great too." Her casual tone aside, Alyce meant it from the bottom of her heart. The three chuckled as they headed for the elevator.

Once inside Peter Brown's office, they were introduced to Roger Murray and Charlie Cole. Alyce assessed them quietly. Both exuded three qualities she appreciated: confidence, efficiency, and self-control.

Roger spoke first. "I am delighted to become a member of your foundation," he said. "Thank you for accepting me. I'll do my best not to disappoint you. I hope my background will be an asset to your group. Permit me to elaborate on my interest in Santanoni."

He settled back into his chair and surveyed the group before speaking. "The Adirondacks are my second home. I go up there to camp and hike as often as I can get away. I've observed the gradual deterioration of Camp Santanoni and it has disturbed me. I've wished there were something I could do to stop it. When Pete called to tell me about your plans, I told him how interested I was in the project. I was pleased when he asked me to join the Foundation to Save Santanoni."

"Thank you, Roger. We're in complete agreement that you should be the fourth member of our group." Bill nodded toward Peter. "Your friend recommends you very highly."

Charlie Cole explained his interest in Santanoni. Alyce could see he'd be an asset to their foundation. The others gave their approval as well.

Peter then handed each a copy of the proposal. "I want you to read your copy again. There's nothing here that wasn't in the copies I gave you last week. I just want to be sure you know what you're agreeing to. We're tackling Goliath, and we need to be fully armed. It's going to take all of your energies and then some to rescue Santanoni."

Alyce wanted to concentrate on the document, but with Bill so near it was hard to focus on the paper in front of her. The fragrance of his citrus aftershave was wreaking havoc with her senses.

"If you have questions, now's the time to get answers before you sign the document. Once you have signed it, my secretary will get the proposal into the hands of the

State Legislature."

Alyce steeled herself against the distracting emotions she was experiencing and began to read each word. She was relieved to have four investors who were willing to help her carry out the wishes of Nellie Hayes. The burden would be much lighter when it was carried by ten hands instead of two.

The names of the five members were listed alphabetically at the end of the document:

> *Alyce Miller Anderson*
> *Charles Edward Cole*
> *William Morgan Hayes*
> *Elisabeth Hayes Montgomery*
> *Roger Lee Murray*

Alyce nodded her head to register her approval of the document. She was about to express her thanks to Peter Brown when suddenly she realized what she had read. Her eyes opened wide and she gasped.

She shot a look at Bill and another at Bette. She didn't want to admit what she was seeing. Bill heard her gasp and turned to face her. He was about to speak when she blurted, "William Morgan Hayes!"

Bette leaped to her feet, her face ashen. She flashed an "I warned you what might happen" look at her big brother.

"And you! Elisabeth Montgomery Hayes!" Alyce's voice shook. It took every ounce of reserve she had to keep from bursting into tears. "I thought you were my friends. That you loved Santanoni. That you wanted to stop the ruin as much as I. You pretended to be my friends to get Santanoni back!" She was almost shrieking.

"Well, friends, it was a nice try but it won't work. You had Santanoni once, but you didn't appreciate it. Your parents died praying for your return. You gave Santanoni up, now don't try to steal it from me. I won't let you have it." Her face was flushed. Her voice cracked, and her tirade ended in sobs.

She threw her copy of the proposal on Peter Brown's desk, snatched her coat from the rack, and bolted out the door. Bill was right behind her.

"Alyce! Alyce! Please come back. Let me explain. You've misjudged us."

By the time Bill made it to the elevator, the door closed in his face. His sister had warned him. Now he had not only lost his opportunity to help restore his old home, but he had lost the only woman he'd ever loved. He shuffled back to the law office. How would he ever explain this?

When he returned to the office, Bette was leaving. She was too angry with Bill to feel sorry for him. Peter and Roger were staring at her.

"Don't look at me that way. Big brother can tell you what a fool he has made of himself in more ways than one! Now I'm going to try to undo some of the damage he's done."

Her eyes hurled more daggers in Bill's direction as she faced him briefly before running to the elevator.

Alyce unlocked her car door with trembling hands. Once inside her seatbelt wouldn't fasten. She was crying so hard, she couldn't see to put the key into the ignition. As she glanced into her rearview mirror, she spotted Bette charging out of the building.

Bette glanced from left to right trying to find her. Alyce eased her car out of her parking place and was swallowed up by the midmorning traffic. She was glad she didn't have to go to work. Her emotions were shattered and right now she couldn't bear to see or talk to anyone. She drove straight home, staggered into her apartment, and slumped into the nearest chair. Though she was still wearing her coat, she was shivering.

Sensing his mistress's distress, Max tried to nuzzle her face, but it was buried under her arm and she pushed him away. *How could she had been such a fool?* After all these years, she should have learned to follow her instincts. Now she knew why Bill looked so familiar. His father had the same brown eyes and a dimpled chin. No wonder Bill knew so much about Santanoni. It was his home.

The one she had trusted had deceived her. She could forgive most wrongs, but she valued truth and honesty. Being the victim of outright deception threw her into a panic.

Her thoughts were interrupted by the phone, but she let it ring. After at least a dozen rings, her head ached from the incessant jangling. In her frustration she grabbed a nearby pillow and threw it at the phone. Finally she got up and removed her coat. She put her hat and scarf away and pondered her next move. There was no use lying down. She wouldn't be able to relax enough to sleep.

She was removing her boots when the doorbell rang. All she asked was to be left alone with her throbbing head and her broken heart. The bell stopped ringing only to be replaced by loud knocking. Alyce did not move.

"Please open the door, Alyce. It's Bette. I must know if you're all right. Just let me see that you are and I promise not to stay."

Realizing she'd get no peace until she did, Alyce opened the door slowly. "I'm okay, Bette," she lied. Her voice broke.

Bette hugged her and both women cried together. "Alyce, please give me a chance to explain. I know we have hurt you deeply, and I regret that. If we could have foreseen what was going to happen, we would have handled things differently. You must hate us both, and with just cause. But there is an explanation."

Alyce stared at her. She did not trust her voice.

Bette pleaded, "Please let me come back tomorrow evening. I'll tell you exactly how this terrible misunderstanding began. Please, Alyce . . .?"

"I don't ever want to see Bill Morgan again . . . or even talk to him." She could not restrain the sobs that shook her shoulders.

thirteen

At seven on the dot the doorbell rang. Alyce, clad in a mint paisley lounging robe, faced Bette in her beautiful mink. Bette's swollen eyes and pale cheeks revealed she had not had an easy day either. With forced politeness, Alyce invited her in.

She took her coat and hung it on a padded hanger in the hall closet. Running her hand over the coat's sumptuous lapels, Alyce thought this was the most gorgeous fur she had ever seen, and Bette had the figure and the finesse to do it justice.

"I've made a pot of herbal tea. Or would you prefer coffee?"

"Tea will be fine, thanks. It was kind of you to let me come. I'm not here to plead my brother's case. I'm here strictly on my own. I know we have hurt you badly."

Alyce listened without comment.

"I'm sorry for that," Bette continued. "I appreciate you as a friend. In California in my circle of friends, or perhaps I should say acquaintances, there are few genuine friendships. The glitter, the glamour, the smiles, they may be broad, but they are only a quarter-inch deep. You're different, Alyce. You're honest and sincere." Still Alyce said nothing and Bette took a deep breath.

"It was a shock to come home and find out my parents were deceased. I was overcome with guilt and remorse. Many years ago, against my parents' wishes, I eloped

123

with my high school art teacher. What I thought was love was mere infatuation. My marriage was a horrible mistake."

She frowned as though she were looking through the wrong end of a telescope and not able to see what she wanted. Finally she went on.

"It took me five years to admit that my husband had married me because of my artistic talent and my family's money. I loved him from the start, and I still love him despite what he did to me. In time he began to abuse me physically. Whatever artistic ability I had was slowly being stifled. I knew I had to get away from him."

She shook her head as if to shake away the unpleasantness of her foolish marriage.

"When I left my husband, I had no money and no place to go. I got a job in a small boutique as a salesperson. The pay was minimal and I struggled to pay my bills. I had always been interested in fashion and secretly I began to design clothing for our customers. I was in my dream world. Sometimes I prepared entire wardrobes on paper for the wealthy women who came to the boutique. Of course, they never saw my work."

She stopped for a sip of tea. Alyce sat in stony silence. She had little interest in Bette's narrative of her personal misfortunes. She wanted to know why Bill had lied about his name.

Bette set her cup down and resumed her narrative.

"One day my boss came to my apartment. He had never been there before, and I was unprepared for guests. He saw my designs strewn about the living room. He praised them and chided me for keeping my talent a secret. He asked to see other things I had designed. After I showed him my notebook, he insisted on sending me to the Venus School of Design so I could develop my talent. When he decided to retire, he sold me his shop at a ridiculously low price. He said it was a gift in appreciation for my hard work for him and his satisfied customers.

"As time went on, I was able to open shops in three more cities. Then about three months ago I collapsed at an opening in Honolulu. My doctor ordered me to take time off and to do absolutely nothing for six weeks."

Alyce wondered why she was telling her all of this. It wouldn't change her mind about Bill.

"Having worked fourteen- to sixteen-hour days for years, I found that was a hard prescription. In addition to that my doctor warned me to give up smoking. I had been a chain smoker for years. Bill and I never kept in touch except on our birthdays, which happened to be the same day. Bill is one year older than I. Somehow we lost contact with each other until an acquaintance of mine returned from Europe having met Bill in Paris. I tracked him down and found out he was going home to Santanoni . . . to see Will and Nellie and to make amends for the years of neglect. Once he had made the decision to return, he couldn't wait to go home."

At the mention of Bill's name, Alyce perked up.

"From the time we became teenagers we called our folks Will and Nellie. Chalk that up to those crazy teen years. Bill asked me to meet him in Newcomb at Thanksgiving so we could go home together. I was busy with my boutiques so I ignored his request. Then when my doctor threatened me with what lay ahead if I continued at my present breakneck pace, I decided to come home."

Alyce was sitting erect now. Thus far the picture Bette had painted did not reveal any sinister secrets that would incriminate Bill or her. They seemed like typical teens with the usual parental clashes. But then she hadn't had time to think about what Nellie had told her about her children. She needed to piece that together with what Bette was saying. Maybe she would find some clues to the present state of events.

"My brother and I both realized, too late unfortunately, that we had been foolish in leaving home against our parents' wishes. We also sorely regretted our stubborn refusals to go back."

Alyce warmed their cups and Bette smiled her thanks. "You're a good listener, Alyce. There is a bit more I need to tell you. Bill met me at the airport in Albany the day before Thanksgiving. We arrived in Newcomb in late afternoon. Seeing how distraught I was, he insisted I have a nap before we talked. Then he met me for dinner. After our meal together, we went back to my room. Bill told me that Will and Nellie were gone and that Santanoni had been sold to the State of New York."

Alyce flinched at the mention of that evening at the Antlers.

"My muddled mind was having such a time comprehending everything I was finding out. Bill tried to console me while also telling me that an attractive nurse from Syracuse had been named executor of Nellie's will. I was angry when he told me about you. I couldn't believe that your befriending my parents was due to nothing but innate kindness on your part. Forgive me, Alyce, but I've lived in the world of dog-eat-dog for a long time. I judged you to have ulterior motives. I was so bitter. I should have been grateful that someone provided Will and Nellie some happiness in their twilight years.

"As Bill talked, I sensed his feelings for you were deep. When I quizzed him, he told me there was a big problem in your relationship, namely that he had not told you who he was. I knew right then he was in trouble. I should have insisted that he get that straightened out. Bill and I were close when we were growing up. I knew that deception would prove disastrous."

As truthful as she believed Bette to be, Alyce flinched at Bill's dishonesty.

"Bill couldn't . . . perhaps because there wasn't any reason he should have lied. True, he was upset when he came home and found Santanoni frequented by hikers and in sad disrepair. Maybe that initial shock caused him to speak so hastily."

Alyce wanted to find some rationale for Bill's behavior so she could forgive him. What would have happened if Bill had told her who he was when they first met? Would that have made any difference in their relationship?

"Alyce, have you ever said something absolutely idiotic and then realized that as soon as the words left your mouth? I think Bill shocked himself. Once he said he was Bill Morgan, he didn't know why he had said it or what to do about it. So he did nothing. That doesn't excuse him, but I think that's what happened."

Alyce thought about that first encounter with Bill. She remembered how he had yelled at Max and at her too. She recalled how tight-lipped he had been about himself after she had rambled on about her life. She had been annoyed with his silence. Now she was beginning to understand. If she could understand, maybe she could forgive him. She remembered assessing him as a wild man in need of a friend.

"I could see how you felt about him. I knew there would be a day of reckoning. I almost told you a couple of times myself. But that would have been interfering with Bill's affairs. I have learned not to be a meddler."

Bette grimaced as though in pain. "I realize now I'm just as guilty as Bill. I'm here to beg your forgiveness for the part I played in this deception. You have every right to be angry with me. I deserve it. Yet, I felt you deserved an explanation."

Bette had hoped for some kind of response from Alyce, any sign that would show she understood. Getting none, she tried once more to make her position clear without defending her brother.

"I'd still like to be a part of the Foundation to Save Santanoni, if you will let me. If you can't forgive me, let me make my contribution as a memorial to Will and Nellie. I owe them so much. I know you love Santanoni as much as Bill and I. Keeping our identities secret was not a calculated move to reclaim Santanoni, though it looks like that. We surrendered our inheritance when we left home many years ago. Can't we work together for the sake of the camp? We need each other."

She hesitated. Then she made one final plea. "Alyce, life doesn't always treat us kindly or fairly. We have to grab happiness wherever it can be found. I know you love Bill even though he has hurt you. I loved my husband too. . . ."

Bette's eyes swelled with tears and Alyce found herself overcome with emotion as well.

"Bill loves you, Alyce. This is the first time in his life

he has been in love. If you can't forgive him right now, will you try to keep your feelings for him separate from your concern for Santanoni? Take as much time as you need to sort out your feelings, but please reconsider the foundation plans. I have to return to California soon. I want to go back knowing there's an active war being waged to save my former home."

Bette rose from her chair and took her cup to the kitchen. She would not stay longer. Alyce got her coat and helped her put it on and together they walked to the door. Bette turned and hugged her. "Thanks for letting me come, Alyce, and thanks for listening."

Alyce nodded and then asked, "Will you stop again before you return to California?"

"Of course I will."

With that she was gone.

fourteen

Wednesday afternoon Alyce took Max for a long walk. The snow had melted and the sidewalks were clear. Since her meeting with Bette, Alyce had put her mind in neutral and kept it there. That was easier than dealing with Bill's lie about his name. She still saw it as an attempt to regain Santanoni. Had she been able to think more rationally, she could have seen the fallacy in her reasoning. She was no threat to Bill when he found her camping on the Santanoni Preserve.

She had scarcely returned to her apartment when the phone rang. Alyce glanced at the clock. It was four-fifteen, a strange time for her to be getting a call. Maybe Peggy needed her again. Sometimes those sneaking viruses lasted longer than usual. She hoped for Peggy's sake that was not the case.

After she answered there was a pause and then a deep, soft voice spoke. "Alyce?" Another pause. "Please don't hang up on me."

Alyce's heart thumped in her throat. She was torn between tears of anger and disbelief. It was she who spoke first, but only a monosyllable. "Yes. . . ."

"I wanted to talk to you sooner, to come to you, to apologize for not telling you the truth. I couldn't come. I kept telling myself if I were in your shoes, I would never want to hear from me again."

Bill's words trickled over her like soap bubbles,

130

tickling her emotions.

"You know I love you. I can't throw away those feelings. I believe you love me too. Remember how you suggested we start our first conversation over again after I barked at you and Max in the woods? Alyce, can't we make another start? I will never deceive you again, so help me, God."

He waited for her answer. The only sound he heard was her soft breath. She was trying to sort out her feelings. Finally she managed a brief sigh.

"What do you expect me to do? Forget the past? That's impossible. Honesty is important to me."

Bill spoke with measured words and his tone held none of the arrogance she recalled from their first meeting. "I hear you, Alyce. Please don't hate me. Will you try to forgive me? I admit I deceived you, and how I regret that. Please try to understand that it was not an attempt to get Santanoni away from you. Alyce, when I met you and Max at Santanoni, I didn't know you had any direct interest in Santanoni other than as a delightful spot for camping out."

Alyce hadn't considered that.

Bill continued. "What can I do to convince you of my sincerity? I've tried to see things from your perspective. You are more important to me than Santanoni. I need your forgiveness. Please give me another chance."

Alyce's mind was in too much turmoil for her to speak.

"I must leave Syracuse for a few months, but I can't go without making peace with you."

She wanted to accept his olive branch but his next comment clipped the thin bough of trust she was hanging on to.

"Of course I still care about Santanoni. I hope you are mature enough to see the necessity of signing the proposal so we can get it to Albany by the time the State Legislature convenes again."

Alyce felt a stab in the pit of her stomach. Bill was still speaking. "I know you want to see the camp restored in memory of Will and Nellie. Can't you set your personal feelings aside so we can get on with saving Santanoni?"

His words rained on her ears like an icy shower. She had the urge to hang up on him, but she knew he would call again. Her head was aching. She might as well hear him out. She hoped he would be quick about it.

Bill's voice was gentle now. "Someday I'll find a way to prove to you my sincerity." He paused. "I'm leaving soon for California and after that I may return to Europe. I'm starting a new book and I need to clear my head."

Still Alyce said nothing.

"You can contact me through Peter Brown's office. Pete will always be able to reach me. Please, Alyce, think about what I've said."

She had to say something to end Bill's monologue. "I'll think about it," she said in a voice devoid of emotion.

"There's one more thing. Please keep in touch with Bette. She needs you. I love you, Alyce." The line went dead.

Alyce stared at the receiver in her hand and carefully put it back in its cradle. She certainly would think. She'd think about a way to erase Bill Morgan Hayes from her life. Once she succeeded at that, she would have to come up with someone else to help her save Santanoni.

Max was sitting by his dish waiting for his supper.

Stooping down she gave him a hug as the tears began to roll down her cheeks. Max was all she had to love, and there was not a deceptive bone in his body.

fifteen

Alyce sat in her lonely apartment on Christmas Eve, a cup of tea in her hands, staring at the small Christmas tree in the corner of her living room. Even Max had deserted her for his favorite spot near the heating vent in the kitchen. She had not heard from Bill, but then she didn't expect to. Why should he call? She was the one who had closed the door on their relationship.

After much painful deliberation she had signed the papers forming the Foundation to Save Santanoni. She would keep the Santanoni issue separate from her relationship with Bill as Bette had suggested. She owed that much to Will and Nellie. Deep down, though, she was doing it for Bill as well.

Life is fleeting and earth's pleasures are not eternal, she reflected, and personal relationships are important. Bill had strained their relationship severely. She knew that. So did he. Could they still be friends? *If we can still be friends,* Alyce thought, *perhaps in time we can become more than friends.*

There on that night set aside to honor God's gift to the world of the Greatest Friend one could ever have, a tiny seed of hope was planted in Alyce's heart. She knelt beside her chair and prayed softly to her Heavenly Father.

"Dear God, please forgive me for the times I've sinned against You. Help me to forgive Bill. Lord, You know I love him. I want to forgive him. But, God, it still hurts so much. With Your help, I'll forgive him and forget the pain I suffered. Thank You, Lord, for forgiving me when I sin against You. In Jesus' name."

A gentle nudge from a cold nose awakened Alyce. She found herself still kneeling by her chair. Max needed to go out. She got up and stretched. She was surprised to see she had been asleep for forty minutes. She arose unaware that the Lord was gently binding up her wounds.

While Max was out she thought about Bette. After some gentle persuasion on Bette's part, they had had lunch together before Bette returned to California. True to her word, there was no mention of Bill or his whereabouts. A few days ago Bette had sent her a beautiful Christmas card. The message was so personal Bette could have composed it herself.

Alyce's thoughts turned again to Bill. *I wonder where he is tonight. I wonder if he is happy. Is he remembering this is the anniversary of Christ's birth? Does he know Jesus? If he doesn't know You, Lord, please, help him to see You in my life. I wonder if he is alone.* She grimaced at the thought of his being with someone else.

A tiny tear crept out of one dark eye and made its way down her cheek. Before long another joined it. She thought she wanted to be alone. Now she regretted that decision. She wiped the tears, picked up her tea cup, and headed for the kitchen.

When the doorbell rang, she glanced at the clock. It was eight-thirty. She wasn't expecting anyone. She looked out the window. A floral delivery van was parked in her driveway. She opened the door.

"Good evening, ma'am. Are you Ms. Alyce

Anderson?"

She nodded.

"A Christmas Eve delivery for you. I'm sorry to be so late, I hope you don't mind." He handed her a large box.

After she thanked him and gave him a generous tip, he bounded down the steps and almost fell as he hit the thin layer of ice that had formed at the bottom. He hopped into his van, slammed the door, and zoomed down the street looking for his next customer. Alyce shook her head and smiled at his youthful exuberance.

She was surprised at the size of the box as she carefully she removed the green bow and ribbon and lifted the lid. Inside were two dozen red roses, cradled in baby's breath and greenery. She counted them again as she delicately removed each one from the box to find the card.

Inside a red envelope was the computer-generated message, "Please give me a second chance. Love, Bill."

Knowing that holidays could be especially hard for Alyce, Bette called on Christmas morning and launched into a lengthy conversation.

When Alyce told her about the lovely flowers from Bill, Bette had little response. They talked of unimportant things until they said their goodbyes. Bette's gentle reminder that Alyce should follow her heart did not fall on deaf ears.

Blustery snowfalls followed Christmas into the new year and then continued to frustrate many a plan as the Syracuse area was blanketed with three feet of snow straight off Lake Ontario.

"It's what we get when the lake doesn't freeze," Alyce reminded her patient. "We've had a warm winter thus far. We're going to keep getting those lake effect storms until Lake Ontario freezes over."

February arrived and so did Valentine's Day. On that day Alyce received more red roses along with a huge box of chocolates. There were two notes with the gifts. The note with the flowers said simply, "I love you, Alyce. Bill." The other note read, "To the sweetest woman in the world."

Alyce was delighted with the gifts, but what she wanted most was to speak to Bill. Bette had sent her a funny valentine and she had called again. She talked of many things, but she never mentioned Bill. Alyce was too proud to ask about him.

March came roaring in and gradually the weather warmed, the pussy willows budded, and people began to smile. Alyce had maintained a busy work schedule, devoting her pent-up passion to her patients. Her heartache over Bill no longer gnawed at her inner being. She still thought about him, but the bitterness was gone. She simply longed to see him. Peter Brown had called several times to let her know how things were proceeding with the Foundation to Save Santanoni, but he too avoided any reference to Bill.

Bette continued to contact her by letter and by phone. They discussed Santanoni and the fact that so far the legislature had not considered their proposal. They both wished they could oil the slow-moving wheels of government.

Alyce ached to know where Bill was and what he was doing. She didn't know how to interpret his gifts since he never called. Unfortunately for both of them, their stubborn pride was keeping them apart. No matter how much

Alyce longed to hear from him, she could not bring herself to ask Bette or Peter where he was. Would she ever conquer her foolish pride?

sixteen

For most of March Alyce continued working days instead of nights. She enjoyed her evenings at home as her mind needed time to be at ease. She read or napped, or thought about the past and wondered about the future. Two questions kept popping into her mind. Would the State Legislature accept their proposal for a Foundation to Save Santanoni? Would she ever see Bill Hayes again?

She was beginning to read the *Post Standard* when the phone jangled. As it was St. Patrick's Day and she was feeling a bit impish, she answered in her best imitation brogue.

"Sure and I'll be wishin' you a good evenin' and a happy St. Paddy's Day."

There was silence on the line while the caller caught his breath. "I beg your pardon. I must have dialed the wrong number. Please excuse me."

Alyce drew in her breath as she heard the click on the other end. If she lived to be 238, she would have recognized that voice. It was Bill and she, trying to be cute, had made him hang up. Her heart was thumping. Her mouth went dry. She swallowed again and again and tears coursed down her cheeks. She had hoped and prayed he'd call. Would he try again?

Her answer came shortly. Brrrrrrrrrrrrrring! Brrrrrrrrrrrrrring!

Now she was giggling through her tears. She let it ring a third time before she answered.

"Hello. . .?"

"Hello, Alyce. This is Bill. Happy St. Patrick's Day."

"Hi, Bill." She felt tongue-tied.

"How are you?"

"Fine." Why couldn't she utter more than one syllable at a time?

"Uh . . . I've missed you . . . I need . . . I want to see you again, Alyce."

She wished her heart would stop hammering in her head. She wanted to get her tongue in gear, but it wouldn't budge. She'd better at least thank him for the flowers. She had been bothered by not knowing how to do that when they first arrived. The seconds ticked by.

"I flew into Hancock Field last night. I'm only here for one day. I called Pete Brown. He has some news about the foundation." He hesitated a moment.

"Alyce, would you be willing to meet with the foundation members at Santanoni during Easter weekend? We need to discuss some specific plans. Perhaps by then the State Legislature will have considered our proposal."

She checked the calendar hanging next to the phone. Finally she found her voice. She hoped it didn't register what she was feeling inside.

"Yes, I can be there. I'll be glad to come." Then she added after a short pause, "I'm glad you called. Thank you for the lovely roses. I had no way to let you know how much I appreciated them."

"The pleasure was mine. I'm glad you liked them. Thanks for being willing to come to Newcomb. Would you like for me to make a reservation for you at the

Antlers?"

"That would be nice. I'm scheduled to work on Maundy Thursday evening. I'll catch some sleep in the morning. I should arrive in time for dinner on Good Friday." As she mentioned dinner, she remembered other dinners at the Antlers. For such an insignificant little inn, it was playing a major role in her life.

"I'll take care of it for you. Goodbye until Easter."

Alyce was crushed. Bill had sounded so glad to hear her voice, but then the conversation was all business. After three months all he had said was that he was glad she liked the roses. He was in Syracuse and he had made no effort to see her. Had the separation convinced him he could live without her? Had he erased her from the secret part of his heart?

She did know that hearing Bill's voice after all those weeks of silence had sent her heart soaring. How she hoped that, somewhere up there in the clouds, his heart would come floating by.

"Good afternoon, Mr. Hayes. It's nice to have you back with us. Will you be staying long?" Matt Flack, a tall thin man with inquisitive black eyes and a shock of gray hair extended his hand with enthusiasm.

"About a week this time, Matt," Bill replied as he signed the guest register at the Antlers. "Ms. Anderson, Charlie Cole, Roger Murray, and my sister Bette will be arriving later this afternoon."

Matt scanned his register. "Oh, yes. We have their reservations, Mr. Hayes."

"Please call me Bill."

"Okay, Bill. I see you're driving an Audi this time

instead of your Lincoln."

Bill smiled inwardly. Matt didn't miss much that was going on around the Antlers. "That was a rental car. Since I intend to stay stateside, I bought my own wheels."

Matt paused and then brought up the subject that was uppermost in his mind whenever he saw Bill. "I have never forgotten what happened to your brother Jimmy. I'm sorry he was never found. This whole community grieved over his disappearance. How we wished we could have found him."

"Everyone tried to find him, Matt. I wonder if he is alive somewhere still." Matt had elicited some painful memories that Bill wasn't anxious to rekindle. He had no desire to discuss the matter with him. His brother's disappearance had produced a chain of painful events that he wished had never happened. He couldn't change the past, but he could concentrate on building a better, happier future.

"Are you planning to make Santanoni your home?" Bill's eyebrows arched at Matt's question.

Before he could answer, Matt went on. "You know how things are in a small town like Newcomb. News travels fast."

"And so do rumors," Bill said under his breath.

"The older folks in town have all been to Santanoni. They talk about how things used to be. As soon as they heard you and your sister were back in the area, there was an upsurge of interest in the camp."

"Hold on a minute, Matt. I'm afraid you are getting carried away with your speculations. Santanoni no longer belongs to our family. It's part of the Adirondack Park." He explained how the Foundation to Save Santanoni had been organized and that they were waiting for movement from Albany. They couldn't proceed with plans for preservation or restoration without official approval.

"Once we secure the blessing of the State Legislature, we can move full steam ahead. Of course our first priority will be to put an end to the deterioration. Then we can think of restoration. It's an expensive proposition. We're going to need help from every possible source we can find. We're hoping you local folks will want to help too."

"You can count on us! The restoration of Santanoni would be a plus for us all." He looked at Bill as if he had just received a divine revelation. "You know you've already increased my business. A number of former residents have heard the rumors and have come back to catch up on the gossip. Those who don't have family in the area stay at the Antlers and pump me for details." His voice reflected his pleasure in reaping the benefits of Bill's plans.

Since people were asking questions, it seemed to Bill a good time to spread some truth to accompany the rumors. "What we have in mind for Santanoni is somewhat like what Howie Kirschenbaum did for Sagamore Camp. We hope we can have as good a program at Santanoni, though we don't plan to duplicate what's already being offered to the public at Raquette Lake."

Since Matt expressed so much interest, Bill went over the tentative pains. The next time someone asked what was going on at Santanoni, he'd have lots to tell. Bill knew this was good publicity for the foundation. The more people knew about their plans, the more apt they would be to help bring them to fruition.

They shook hands and Bill picked up his bag. He needed to get to his room and get settled before the others arrived.

"Thanks for sharing your plans, Bill. I wish you the best of luck in seeing them realized. We're happy to have you home again. Let us know how we can help, from fund raising to elbow grease. I can post notices on my walls anytime and most of the town folks will read them."

As he unpacked his belongings, Bill thought that this weekend was off to a good start. That boded well for the next few days. Now if only he could regain the ground he had lost with Alyce. He'd lived through four months of agony when he didn't have the nerve to contact her. How he hoped she had been able to forgive him. He whistled to himself as he hung up his jacket.

There was something about her personality that made Alyce Anderson special, and different from other women he had dated. He was first aware of it that Thanksgiving Sunday when he had gone to church with her. Was it her high-minded principles. . .or the light that shone from her eyes when she smiled at him? Suddenly he realized what he perhaps had known from the moment he met her. Alyce was a Christian. As a new believer, and because of his peripatetic wanderings, Bill hadn't had much chance to meet unattached Christian women.

Bill dropped to his knees by the bed and buried his head in his hands. "Dear Lord," he prayed, "thank You for bringing me back home again, and thank you most of all for leading me to Alyce. Now I know for sure that she is a gift from You. Please direct my words so that in time she will forgive me, if this is Your will. I ask this in Jesus' name. Amen."

seventeen

No sunshine heralded the day as the foundation members squeezed into Charlie Cole's four-wheel drive and headed toward the Santanoni gatehouse. The soggy morning was the fallout from a twelve-hour rainfall. They were in for a muddy hike. Undaunted, they had come equipped with notepads, levels, measures, and protective raingear. Only after they determined how extensive the deterioration was to the buildings could they begin to estimate the costs for restoring and preserving the great camp.

The five had enjoyed a pre-Easter supper together at the Antlers. The cook, having been made privy to their plans for the following day, packed them a lunch and they found it waiting for them along with thermoses of coffee and tea at the front desk when they left the inn that morning. The only complaint came from Bill, the most seasoned hiker in the lot, who wished the abundant provisions had not been stowed away in a large picnic basket.

They parked at the gatehouse and each collected his personal possessions. "I wish I had my backpack with me," said Bill.

Charlie eyed the lunch and then spoke up. "I think the old pack I used to take fishing is under the seat. I'm not sure what it smells like, but a little fish odor might be easier to carry than a picnic basket." He poked around under the seat until he found it.

Alyce signed them in at the register. It was such a natural thing for her to do, but she missed having Max with her. They had not gone far when a raccoon ran across their path. "Too bad you didn't bring Max with you, Alyce. He'd have warned us that we had company."

Bill's comment was music to her ears. She smiled as she explained to Charlie and Roger that Max was her boxer dog as well as her camping companion. Everyone laughed and the trip began on a light-hearted note despite the soggy weather.

Alyce was thinking her own thoughts as they sloshed along. They weren't about Max, as much as he would have enjoyed being there with them. She was telling herself she had been right in forgiving Bill. She remembered the passage she had read in her Bible the previous night, the one in which Jesus had told a crowd of accusers that the one who was without sin should cast the first stone. One by one the men slipped away. When the last accuser had fled and Jesus was alone with the woman, He offered her forgiveness. "Go and leave your life of sin," He said.

Alyce knew at that moment she had forgiven Bill. His reason for lying about his name was no longer important. Together they would restore Santanoni. It would be a memorial to loved ones from their past as well as a monument to their future.

Then a cloud of doubt hovered over her. She had forgiven Bill, but he had not made any direct moves to renew their relationship. After his four months' absence, his contact with her had been strictly a business arrangement. That thought disturbed her as she tramped along behind him on the muddy path. She'd better not let him

know how much she cared about him. She was still trying to figure out why he left the area so abruptly last
December.

By the time they reached the lodge, the sky was clear-
ing. Bill suggested they enjoy their lunch first since it
was nearly noon and then they could work uninterrupted
until they finished. They sat on the lodge steps overlooking Newcomb Lake and feasted on the bountiful provisions.

As the sun broke through the clouds they headed down
to the boathouse. The studio would be next on their agenda
and, if time permitted, they would take a look at the lodge.
They knew they would need the services of a restoration
architect, but they wanted a rough idea of the extent of
the damage before they approached someone with the
job.

Bette volunteered to be the scribe. Alyce would hold
the tape as Bill took measurements to see how much the
building's foundation had settled. Meantime Charlie and
Roger would check the windows to see what they needed.
Alyce was delighted to be paired with Bill. She wondered whose idea that was.

Bill was smiling as he handed her the tape. Did his
hand linger a moment longer than necessary as she took
it from him?

Part of the floor inside the boathouse was rotted away.
Bill glanced up at the roof. Rain and melting snow had
leaked through. The roof was in bad shape.

Charlie and Roger found three of the windows needed
new glazing and one of the sills needed to be replaced.
One pane was missing and the opening had been boarded
up. Boarded-up windows bothered Alyce. They seemed

like someone who used to care didn't anymore. Was that how Bill felt about her?

The large doors that opened to allow the small boats to be loaded and unloaded were in good shape. The cables that operated them were rusty but a good cleaning and oiling would make a big difference.

"I think we'd better take a look at the roof next," Bill said.

Not having a ladder available, Bill scaled the blue spruce that grew flush with the right side of the building. He was careful to choose thick, strong branches that would not be harmed by his weight. Gingerly he picked his way across the sloping roof that was covered with a thick layer of soggy leaves and pine needles. He placed each foot carefully, testing every spot before letting his weight rest on it. His rubber boots gave him sure footing, but there was no way of knowing the condition of the roof under the debris.

As Bill picked his way across, he examined the edge and then worked his way up to the top. The heavy build-up of pine needles had weakened the roof. He tried shoving them off with his feet as he crept along.

Bette cautioned him, "Be careful, Bill. We don't want to carry you back to the gatehouse."

Her words were lost as the roof under Bill gave way. An ominous sound of splintering wood was followed by Bill's cry. There was a sickening thud and then silence.

Bill lay on his left side on the floor of the boathouse. Alyce reached him first. She knelt beside him and unbuttoned his shirt to feel his carotid pulse in his neck. Even as she checked his pulse, she prayed his injuries were not serious.

Dear God, she prayed silently, *I pray he hasn't broken his neck or injured his spinal cord. I love him so much, and I've never told him I forgive him. Maybe I'll never have the chance. Please, God, help him. Even if he must be paralyzed, don't take him away from me. I'll take care of him no matter what condition he is in.*

Her nursing skills in full play, she felt his pulse, faint as it was. She was determined not to cry.

"We need to get him on his back, Charlie. I'll steady his head and neck. Lift him as gently as you can."

Together they straightened him out on Bette's raincoat. Bill moaned. His eyelids fluttered. "My arm feels like an elephant sat on it." His voice was faint.

Alyce could see his arm was broken. When she touched it just below the elbow, he groaned again. It was already beginning to swell.

"Try to lie still, Bill. I need to see where else you're hurt."

Pain blotted out the gentle probing of Alyce's hands. Having determined there were no more serious injuries, Alyce asked Bill to try to stand. With Charlie and Roger on either side of him, he was able to get to his feet. Gingerly he took a few steps. Though shaken and weak, he seemed to be all right except for his arm.

Alyce removed his jacket from his swollen arm and wrapped it around his shoulder. She didn't want him to get chilled. She looked around. "We need something for a sling until we can get you to the emergency room."

Bette offered the warm scarf she had been wearing. Using the scarf and the strap from Charlie's fishing pack, Alyce fashioned a sling to hold the broken arm in place. Her hands trembled as she secured Bill's injured arm in the makeshift sling. She must not let him know how badly his fall frightened her.

"We'll get you to the hospital as quickly as we can, Bill." She winced as she thought of the five miles that separated them from their vehicle. It would be a long walk and there was nothing she could give Bill for the pain. She offered him a weak smile. "Do you think you can make it?" Charlie and Roger were supporting him as he struggled to the door of the boathouse.

Bill grimaced with each step. He looked at his companions. "Looks like I'll have to, doesn't it? I'd freeze to death if I stayed here."

A prayer of thanksgiving winged its way heavenward as Alyce and Bette watched the three men make their way out the door. The restoration of Santanoni would have to wait a little longer.

Meantime Bette and Alyce picked up Charlie's pack and the other things the group had brought with them. Most everything fit into the empty pack. It was inconvenient not having the strap, but they would take turns carrying it back to the gatehouse.

When they had gone about halfway, Charlie ran ahead to get the vehicle. "I'll have it warm and I'll see if I can't drive in as far as the barn. I can turn around there. That'll save Bill some walking."

Alyce handed the fishing pack to Bette and took Charlie's place at Bill's side. She hoped he couldn't feel her racing heart as she encircled him with her right arm and continued to lift him to the Lord in prayer.

Black clouds were again forming overhead. Bette watched them scud across the sky. She frowned. Then she voiced what each one had been thinking. "I hope it holds off until we get Bill safely inside."

"It will!" Alyce's tone was determined.

When the barn was in sight, they cheered when they saw Charlie and transportation waiting for them. Carefully Alyce and Roger eased Bill into the back seat. Alyce climbed in and sat beside him, willing him to bear the pain until they could get him relief.

As they headed back to the gatehouse, she laid her hand on his head and whispered, "I'm sorry we don't have anything for the pain, Bill." She would gladly have borne it for him had there been a way. Bill understood. He took her hand and gave it a feeble squeeze. Then he closed his eyes and gritted his teeth.

Alyce remained with Bill as his arm was X-rayed and set in a cast. The attending doctor administered a strong painkiller. Bill was insistent that he not be admitted to the hospital. The doctor acquiesced when he learned Alyce was a nurse. However, he warned Bill of the consequences of not taking it easy until the arm as well as the rest of his bruised body had healed.

Alyce put her arm around Bill's waist to steady him as they left the emergency room. He responded by squeezing her gently with his uninjured hand. She gazed up at him and met a weak smile.

"Alyce, I love you with all of my heart. I know I could never get along without you. Today proved it. Will you marry me?"

The relief of Bill's being able to go home and then the suddenness of his proposal left Alyce speechless. Did she hear him correctly? Or was she dreaming? She was used to patients being so grateful that they made rash promises as soon as they began to feel better. Bill didn't

know what he was asking. She didn't know whether to
laugh or to cry. By the time they reached the waiting
room, she was doing both, and she had not answered Bill's
question. Her friends welcomed them with applause.

No one had much to say as they drove back to the Antlers. Bill dozed, thanks to the sedative he had been given.
Alyce was enduring almost as much mental turmoil as
Bill was suffering physically as she wrestled with his proposal. As much as she wanted to believe he meant it, she
attributed the question to his accident and his being over-
wrought.

She bowed her head and prayed silently. *Lord, thank
You that Bill did not break his neck in the accident. Thank
You for helping us get him to the hospital. Please heal
his bruises and his broken arm. Lord, You know I love
him. I don't know if he loves me. Please, God, help me
know what I should do.*

eighteen

Bill and Bette had to return to California by the end of the week and Alyce volunteered to drive them to Hancock Field. Once again she found herself battling inner turmoil as Bill sat beside her enroute to the airport. Did he really want to marry her? She wanted to believe he did, but she was afraid to. She wished she could put her finger on the cause for her doubts. She had been in love with him for a long time, and the months he was away had been painful for her.

Bill would be expecting an answer before he left the airport. She had to tell him something. *Please God, help me know what I should say,* she sent heavenward desperately.

She had seen Bill only once since his accident, and that had been in the presence of others. His searching eyes pleaded for a positive response at that meeting, but she was not able to give it to him. They would soon be parting. Did she or didn't she trust Bill Hayes?

At the airport Alyce was surprised to see that Charlie Cole had come to say goodbye. She made a mental note that Bette, on the other hand, seemed unusually pleased to see him.

When their flight to San Francisco was announced, Alyce hugged Bette and urged her to write as soon as she got home.

"Do us both a big favor and marry my brother," Bette

whispered as they embraced. "He's too miserable to function without you. Alyce, you are the first woman he has ever wanted to marry."

"Don't rush me, Bette. Try those designer wedding gowns on your California brides until I make up my mind."

Then Bill was holding her and the world around her disappeared. He gazed into her eyes seeking an answer. "Will you, Alyce?"

She looked long into those intense dark eyes, but she didn't speak. Bill's farewell kiss left no doubt in her mind that he wanted her and needed her.

"I'll wait as long as I have to," he whispered. "I love you with all of my heart."

He released her and joined Bette at the boarding gate. Alyce stayed on the observation deck until their plane was airborne and then out of sight.

As Alyce drove back to her apartment, she pondered her indecision. She didn't enjoy fighting invisible dragons. She was reminded of some verses of Scripture from a sermon she had heard on the radio. "Dear Lord, You have told us that if any man lacks wisdom, let him ask of God who giveth to all men liberally. Well, I'm asking, Lord, because that's what I need. Wisdom."

She thought about Gideon, a Bible character with whom she could surely identify. The Lord had reduced his mighty army to 300 and then told him to go fight. Gideon wanted proof of the Lord's presence. So he tested Him twice. Each time the Lord honored his test. Gideon went forth with his little army and his trust in the Lord and he gained a great victory.

It was time to ask the Lord for His direct intervention

in her life. "Father in heaven," she prayed, "I need Your assurance just as Gideon did. You know I love Bill. He says he loves me, and I believe him. Yet I have doubts about marrying him. Father, please remove my doubts. Make something happen to show me that Bill and I are to marry. Or," she hesitated a few seconds, "show me clearly that we should not. In Jesus ' name."

The legislative hearings were set for the first of June and the Santanoni proposal was on the agenda. Senator McKunckle had informed the attorney's office all was in order for the presentation. He would ask for approval of Phase I. That would provide for the formation of a non-profit foundation to restore the existing buildings and manage them exclusively for educational and recreational purposes. Any changes in the policies governing the Adirondack Park had to be approved by two consecutive legislative assemblies. After that the proposal would be submitted to the voting public.

Peter Brown was delighted and he quickly relayed the news to each of the members of the proposed foundation. Roger was the last member he called. It took several days to reach him. Finally he was able to speak to him and tell him what was happening in Albany. He waited for Roger's response, expecting him to be as enthusiastic as the others.

"I hate to tell you this, Pete, but I have a big problem," Roger said tentatively when he finally got through to Pete. "That's why I've been away. I'll spare you the nasty details, but I'm going to have to withdraw from the foundation before we get started. I'm sorry, but the funds I was counting on to invest in this camp did not materialize."

Pete's mind was racing ahead. Where could they find a replacement in such a short time?

"I'm terribly embarrassed about the situation, but I can't come up with $100,000. My heart is with you and your plans for Santanoni, but you need cash that I can't provide."

"Roger, I'm sorry too. I'll explain the situation to the others. They'll be disappointed, of course, but I'm sure they'll understand. Let me know if your situation changes."

Pete dictated letters to the others explaining the latest snag in their plans. He would wait for suggestions for a replacement for Roger. He hoped they'd be able to find someone by the time the legislative hearings began. If approval were granted to form the foundation, they could speed up their plans.

When Bill received word of Roger's financial dilemma, he sent a telegram to Pete telling him to proceed with the plans. He would provide the $100,000 they were expecting from Roger.

A week later when Bette called Alyce to discuss the upcoming hearings, Alyce commented, "I'm glad we're finally going to get a hearing, but I'm worried about a replacement for Roger."

"Don't worry, Alyce. With four of us looking, we should find somebody in due time."

"But what's due time? If we get legislative approval and don't have our replacement, we'll be $100,000 short. What's that going to tell those lawmakers?"

"That's no problem. When Bill heard about Roger's pulling out, he wired Pete telling him he would put in the extra $100,000."

Alyce couldn't believe it. Or rather, she didn't want to believe what Bette was saying. By adding that money, Bill and Bette controlled three-fifths of the foundation.

"Alyce? Alyce? Are you still there?"

"I'm here, Bette. Thanks for calling." With slow, deliberate movements, she put the phone back into its cradle and burst into tears. *Well, Lord, I guess I have my answer.* It wasn't the one she wanted, but she would accept it.

Alyce stared into space. Bill had acted without consulting her and that hurt. But it bothered her more to learn that he was so wealthy he could fling down another $100,000. That he had concealed his wealth was disturbing. She was not a rich woman, and she didn't want to be one.

"Lord, I asked You for a sign. I hoped it was Your will for me to marry Bill. I can't marry someone I don't trust." She blew her nose and continued her prayer. "Lord, You know how much I hurt. Please take away the pain. Help me give Bill the gift of forgiveness. I know You have a plan for my life, and for his life too. Show me the plans You have for me and I'll follow them. That's the only way I'll find peace."

After thrashing her way through a long night, Alyce got up early and composed her long overdue letter to Bill.

> *Dear Bill,*
>
> *I'm sorry. My answer is no.*
>
> *Alyce*

Two could be as silent as one, she reasoned, as she sealed the envelope with trembling hands. Later that day she made a quick decision to attend a conference in Atlanta. Spring would already have arrived there and she'd enjoy the flowers. The conference would last three days. Then she'd take two more days to enjoy the sights.

By the time Bill received her note, she would be winging her way south. Since Bill wouldn't know where she was, he couldn't call to demand an explanation. She grimaced. She knew the time would come when she'd have to explain, but she refused to think about that now.

Alyce returned home refreshed. Springtime in Atlanta was beautiful and the conference had proved stimulating. She could go on without Bill. In time she'd look back on their relationship as another one of those experiences that made life interesting. She'd bury herself in her work again. There were countless hurting people who needed love and attention and she'd give it to them.

She had been home only three hours when she received a frenzied call from Bette.

"Alyce, what in the world is going on between you and Bill? We're both frantic. We've been trying to reach you ever since Bill got your letter. Are you ill? Ever since you wrote, Bill has been behaving like a madman."

Alyce knew exactly what Bette meant. Hadn't she witnessed that behavior the first time she and Bill met? It was no concern of hers how he was acting. She would be kind to Bette because she liked her, but that would not change her relationship with him.

"I'm sorry, Bette, but Bill and I no longer have a relationship. How he acts is no concern of mine."

"What are you talking about? I thought you two were about to announce your engagement."

"I'm afraid not, not now or any other time." It was hard for Alyce to get those words out. Each one was painful, but they needed to be uttered. Speaking them out loud seemed to finalize her decision.

There was a pause as Bette absorbed what Alyce had said. "You aren't going to marry my brother?" The way she asked it brought Alyce to the brink of tears.

"No, I'm not," she responded with a quiver in her voice.

"Alyce, please tell me why. Forgive me for prying, but you're so suited to each other. You both know what you want and you're both fighters. Bill wouldn't give me your reason for rejecting him. He went storming off to Brussels saying he had business to attend to and he didn't know when he'd get back. I know you both. Neither one of you will be happy without the other. What is this foolishness anyway?"

Alyce was annoyed. She liked Bette, but this matter was between her and Bill. She didn't feel she needed to explain. "Look, Bette. Bill didn't give you any reason because I didn't give him one. If he wants to pursue the matter, that's his privilege. I'm sorry, but I don't wish to discuss it now. Thank you for calling. I hope you and I can still be friends."

Later that evening as Alyce prepared for bed the phone rang again. She glanced at the clock wondering who would be calling at that hour. She had scarcely said hello when Bill interrupted her.

"Alyce, what on earth is going on? Are you ill? Your letter was so curt. What do you mean your answer is no?

You can't tell me you don't love me. Why are you refus-
ing me? I love you, and I know you love me. I saw it in
your eyes. I felt it when I held you in my arms. What has
happened?"

With tears cascading down her cheeks, she opened her
mouth three times before words would come. Her heart
was in her throat. She felt her breath being squeezed from
her lungs. "I didn't think I owed you an explanation,
Bill. You haven't been too free about giving explanations to me."

"What on earth are you talking about?" He felt her sigh
and sensed her anguish all the way to Brussels.

"I'm talking about your latest covert activity," she said
through clenched teeth. "You might have consulted me
before adding more of your abundant wealth to the Foundation to Save Santanoni. It is my project, or did you
forget that?"

"Oh, Alyce. Is that the problem? My dear, you don't
understand. I had to put the money up front so we could
keep moving. Once we have a replacement for Roger,
I'll withdraw it. It wouldn't have been right for me to let
our plans flounder while we search for a new member.
Santanoni is too important to all of us for that. It was my
way of helping."

"I agree, Bill. It would help a lot to have three-fifths
of the foundation's funds provided by the Hayeses. It
would be convenient to have three-fifths of the votes when
issues come up, wouldn't it?"

Bill's mind was racing as he tried to see things from
Alyce's perspective.

"Bill, if and when I marry again it will be to someone
whom I trust completely. Marriage must be based on

openness and trust between husband and wife."

Bill's frustration was reaching the danger point. "Alyce, I promised you I would never deceive you again. I've kept that promise. I love you. I want you. I need you. If I have to give up my interest in Santanoni to prove my love for you, I'm willing to do that."

He paused for a quick breath.

"I'm flying home to San Francisco on Monday. I'll be there for three weeks. Please reconsider. You can call me at Bette's house. If I don't hear from you, I promise I'll get out of your life. I'll withdraw my interest in Santanoni and turn the whole thing over to you and Pete and Bette."

Alyce blanched at Bill's ultimatum. She didn't know how to respond.

"There's nothing more I can say. I love you enough to respect your wishes. If you close the door on me this time, I won't knock again. Good night, darling."

There was a soft click and then silence.

nineteen

The days dragged by and the nights plodded along behind them. Alyce was oblivious to her surroundings. No matter how busy she kept herself in the daytime, she couldn't get a good night's rest. Whenever she closed her eyes, she envisioned Bill, phone in hand, issuing his ultimatum. *If you close the door on me this time, I won't knock again.* Over and over the words echoed through her head until she wanted to scream.

When she got that scene out of her mind, others took its place. Dinner at Sylvia's. Their surprise meeting with Robert Roberts. Bill finding her at Santanoni. And most frightening, Bill's fall at the boathouse. Her heart beat faster as she relived that accident. The possibility that Bill had been seriously injured had made her realize how much she loved him.

After tossing and turning for hours, Alyce got up and made a cup of herbal tea. She patted Max when he came into the kitchen to keep her company. "Oh, Max, whatever am I going to do?"

Max focused his liquid brown eyes on her as if to say, "Don't worry. Things will turn out all right."

She set her cup on the table. Her eyes filled with tears remembering her gift of red roses. It had been two weeks since Bill had called from Brussels. Her time was running out.

During her restless nights she had replayed his final

words over and over in her mind. *I had to put the money up front so we could keep moving while we find a replacement for Roger . . . It wouldn't have been right to let our plans flounder . . . . Santanoni is too important for that . . . If I do not hear from you, I'll get out of your life . . . I love you too much to ignore your wishes.*

"Lord, what am I going to do?"

She picked up her Bible and began to turn pages. When she was troubled, she found comfort in leafing through the Scriptures and reading those passages she had underlined. If she read long enough, she usually found a verse or two that helped her with her current crisis.

> THE LORD God said, "It is not good for the man to be alone. I will make a helper suitable for him ." So the LORD God caused the man to fall into a deep sleep; and while he was sleep- ing, he took one of the man's ribs and closed up the place with flesh. Then the LORD God made a woman from the rib he had taken out of the man, and he brought her to the man. For this reason a man will leave his father and mother and be united to his wife, and they will become one flesh.*

Alyce read the passage a second time. God did not intend for man to live alone. Could it be He did not intend for her or for Bill Hayes to live alone? The last time she and Bill had attended church, hadn't she been positive he shared her faith? Had God been preparing them for each other?

*Genesis 2:18-24 (assorted verses) (NIV).

She recalled Bill's conversation once more, his determination to find out why she had refused him, his explanation which she now realized was sensible. She had been concerned with having to tell the state legislators they had lost a member of their proposed foundation along with $100,000 in support. Instead of being infuriated, she should have been grateful that Bill had the foresight to see the money needed to be available at once.

Again she had jumped to a false conclusion.

Her mind continued its racing, but things were making sense. There was one more obstacle. Bill was a rich man. He had grown up surrounded by wealth, and now in his own business and his writing he had continued to be successful. A lack of funds would never be a problem for him. Alyce was reared in a frugal household. Would her thrifty ways embarrass him? Would he be ashamed of her as he got to know her better?

She picked up her Bible again. She was grateful that her aunt had raised her in a Christian home. She turned to the thirteenth chapter of First Corinthians, the love chapter, and scanned it. She had parts of it memorized, so it didn't take long to find the verses she was looking for. "Love is patient . . . It is not self-seeking . . . It keeps no record of wrongs."

"Forgive me, Lord," she prayed. "I've been keeping a record that needs to be erased. Teach me to forgive even as You have forgiven me."

She read on. "Love never fails." That was the assurance she needed. She knew she loved Bill despite the real and imaginary hurts she had experienced. Though she didn't always understand him, she loved him and she knew he loved her . . . so much that he would stay away if that's what she wanted. She could entrust her future to him.

She glanced at the clock, calculated what time it would be in San Francisco, and picked up the phone. She couldn't wait another minute before calling Bill. Her hand trembled as she dialed Bette's number.

"Hello?" Bette peered at the clock on her nightstand. Who on earth was calling her at that frightful hour?

"Bette, this is Alyce." Bette would not have recognized the soft, restrained voice.

"Alyce! How are you? Is something wrong?"

"Nothing's wrong. Well, yes, lots of things are wrong. I mean. . . . Oh, please let me talk with Bill."

Bette smiled. She hoped the call meant Alyce had had a change of heart. "Just a minute. I'll go wake him up."

The past few days Bill had tried to ignore her whenever possible, or offered curt replies to the few questions she'd asked. Bette knew what was bothering him and she had tried to be patient. She hoped Alyce's call would return him to civility. At least it was a move in the right direction.

There was a fumbling of the phone and then Bill spoke. "Alyce. I was beginning to lose hope."

Tears were streaming down her cheeks. She knew what she was doing was right, yet she struggled for words. "Oh, Bill. I've been so miserable without you. I need to see you, to talk with you, to let you hold me in your arms."

Bill felt he should pinch himself to make sure this conversation was really taking place. "Darling, do you really mean that?"

"Yes, oh, yes, I do. I haven't been able to sleep for days. I'm so sorry I misjudged you. You love me. You've done what you could to prove your love. You gave more than your share to keep the Santanoni proposal intact, and I criticized you for that. I've wronged you. I'm so sorry. Please forgive me."

"Of course I forgive you. You've just made me the happiest man in the state of California! How I wish I could be there to hold you and to kiss away those tears."

"I'm sorry I hurt you. Please come to Syracuse."

"Darling, I'd be there tonight if it were possible but it's not. I have several commitments here for the next few weeks." He held the phone in one hand and rummaged for his pocket calendar. "How about spending the Fourth of July weekend with me at Santanoni? We could return to the Antlers and take day trips backpacking into the camp." He found himself chuckling. "You could even bring Max."

Alyce was feeling light-headed. "We'd both enjoy that! Bill, I'm sorry that I called you at such a ridiculous hour. Once I made up my mind it was the thing to do, I couldn't wait another minute. Please forgive me."

Bill laughed. "Promise me you'll never change. I love you, darling. I'm glad you called. I'll see you soon. We have a lot to talk about."

Alyce sighed with pleasure and relief as she hung up the phone. She gave Max a hug and danced into her bedroom. In her dreams she and Bill strolled arm in arm through the restored lodge at Santanoni.

Alyce and Max arrived at the gatehouse shortly before noon. Bill had left a note for her at the trailhead to meet him farther down the trail. He had signed it, "I love you, Bill."

As she signed the trail register, she smiled with anticipation. This time she didn't have to sign Max's name. She had another protector awaiting her.

Alyce was too excited to appreciate the early spring flowers as she hurried along. She did not have long to wait. As she rounded the bend near the barn, she saw Bill standing beside the old milkhouse. His back was toward the path as he appraised the structure, so he did not see her approaching. She could scarcely contain herself. Soon she would be in his arms. *How I love him!* she thought ecstatically. *How good God is to bring us together.*

Max spied his old friend and scampered to him with his stubby tail twitching wildly. Bill turned to face her and Alyce paused, drinking him in. They looked long at each other and then Bill smiled and held out his arms to receive her.

They clung to each other as if their clinging would erase all the hurt and misunderstanding, all that would ever come between them. Bill kissed away her tears as he hugged her to his chest. He knew they were tears of joy and they mingled with his own.

Finally he released her. "Let's walk down by the lake and we can talk there."

They hiked hand in hand into the lodge, stopping often to embrace in the warm sun. "I just can't hold you enough," Bill whispered in her ear.

While Max made his usual investigations they walked down to the beach and sat in the sun. Bill drew Alyce to him. "I want you to know something I should have told you months before. A short time ago I dedicated my life to the Lord. You have always been so forthcoming about your faith, and I, well, I'm just starting to feel confident about expressing myself. I do know that the Lord has brought us together, and together we can . . ." He paused and cupped his hands around her face. "Alyce, do you still want to marry me?"

"Yes!" she whispered. She had never been surer in her life. Together they would create a Christian home, and together their marriage would be forever sustained by the Lord.

Bill hugged her again. He reached into his pocket and pulled out a small gold box. He opened it and removed a one-carat diamond solitaire ring and slipped it on her finger.

As Alyce stared at the ring, tears welled up in her eyes. "Thank you, darling," she whispered. "I will treasure it forever."

"I think it's time we made some wedding plans, don't you?"

Alyce nodded. "Since it all began right here, wouldn't it be nice to be married at the lodge? Maybe someday we could make Santanoni our home."

"Home for me will always be wherever you are, but I like the idea of being married here. Max can come to the wedding!"

They laughed and hugged and then Bill reached into his pocket again. "I have something else for you." He handed her a sealed letter. It was addressed to the Foundation to Save Santanoni; the return address was the New York State Senate.

"Pete forwarded the letter to me at the Antlers. I wanted us to open it together."

Alyce looked into his eyes as she took the letter. With trembling hands she ran her forefinger under the seal and then removed the contents. Her eyes opened wider as she scanned the page, then she threw her arms around him. "Oh, Bill! Listen to this!"

A Letter To Our Readers

Dear Reader:

In order that we might better contribute to your reading enjoyment, we would appreciate your taking a few minutes to respond to the following questions. When completed, please return to the following:

Rebecca Germany, Editor
Heartsong Presents
P.O. Box 719
Uhrichsville, Ohio 44683

1. Did you enjoy reading *Music in the Mountains*?
   ☐ Very much. I would like to see more books by this author!
   ☐ Moderately
   I would have enjoyed it more if _____

   _____

2. Are you a member of *Heartsong Presents*? Yes   No
   If no, where did you purchase this book? _____

   _____

3. What influenced your decision to purchase this book? (Circle those that apply.)

Cover	Back cover copy
Title	Friends
Publicity	Other _____

4. On a scale from 1 (poor) to 10 (superior), please rate the following elements.

___Heroine   ___Plot

___Hero   ___Inspirational theme

___Setting   ___Secondary characters

5. What settings would you like to see covered in *Heartsong Presents* books?

_____

_____

6. What are some inspirational themes you would like to see treated in future books?_____

_____

_____

7. Would you be interested in reading other *Heartsong Presents* titles?   Yes   No

8. Please circle your age range:

Under 18	18-24	25-34
35-45	46-55	Over 55

9. How many hours per week do you read? _____

Name _____

Occupation _____

Address _____

City _____ State _____ Zip _____